WHITE
for a
SHROUD

WHITE
for a
SHROUD

DONALD CLOUGH
CAMERON

COACHWHIP PUBLICATIONS
Greenville, Ohio

For listening to the thousand recollections and speculations from which it was made . . . for sharing the drudgery of writing without benefit of those obscure satisfactions which beguile authors from more honest toil . . . for playing the difficult role of the critic on the hearth with gracious sincerity—and most of all for reasons that have little to do with reason, being grounded in affection—this book is gratefully dedicated

To Eva

White for a Shroud, by Donald Clough Cameron
© 2023 Coachwhip Publications edition
Cover: Snow (Zaphad1, CC BY 2.0)
https://creativecommons.org/licenses/by/2.0/

First published 1947
Donald Clough Cameron, 1905-1954
CoachwhipBooks.com

ISBN 1-61646-569-7
ISBN-13 978-1-61646-569-8

1

It was a blizzard. The wind got its start somewhere in Canada and came lashing down a hundred and fifty miles across Lake Superior, churning the open water to angry spray that froze while it leaped, buckling the four-foot shore ice with ear-stunning thunder and thrusting it high and dry on land. The snow was an aerial avalanche of glassy points that danced and hissed; it piled up stream-lined mountains in the lee of ridges, higher than the ridges themselves; it choked highways and ditches and the streets of towns, blotted out railroads and rose like floodwater in the Upper Michigan forests.

Andrew Brant sat in the untidy front office of the Red Rock *Reporter* and scowled at a typewriter that had seen better days. A two-inch curtain of solid ice and snow covered the plate-glass windows facing the street, shutting out what little daylight was left. Above Brant's head a dangling electric bulb, green-shaded, showered down a yellow glare which emphasized in highlight and shadow the hewn-granite plainness of his features—the hazel eyes, set deep in their sockets, the broad and prominent nose, the wide mouth and square chin. His hair was black and coarse and rumpled. He was of medium height, stocky and muscular, and his age was twenty-eight.

His blunt forefingers poised above the bank of discolored keys, pounced and wrote:

> *Once again Red Rock faces complete isolation. Prisoners of a storm that may rank with the worst on record, we 1,300-odd men, women and children will be utterly alone and interdependent. In the next five days fire, flood or human cussedness might destroy the rest of the world, and we be none the wiser. And if human cussedness, flood or fire should destroy us, the world would never know until—*

Carol Johnson said, "We need more fire, Andy."

He transferred his scowl to a desk at the other side of the office. "Why don't you put on more clothes? What have you got under that dress?"

"Only a cad would ask a lady such a question, you cad." She grinned and Brant grinned back at her. Carol had an engaging grin that made a pleasing contrast with the demure gravity with which it alternated. She was slim and pretty, with gold-brown hair and gray-blue eyes, and was seven years younger than Brant.

She had been a gawky kid in pigtails when he left Red Rock six years ago to work on newspapers in Detroit and Chicago. He had not seen her on his infrequent visits since, possibly because those visits concerned another girl. But the other girl had married another man, and when Brant returned two weeks ago to buy the *Reporter,* which had been thrown on the market by the death of old Chuck Lyman, he found Carol grown up and ambitious to become either a reporter or an author of highbrow novels—she wasn't sure which until he offered her a job. As society editor, star reporter, advertising manager and secretary to the publisher she constituted the entire office staff of the *Reporter*, and earned every penny of her salary.

Brant pushed back his chair, got up and pried open the hinged cover of the stove. He emptied half a scuttle of coal into its maw, closed the lid and stirred the fire at the bottom of the grate with a poker. The stove chuckled and ticked like a watch, and the heat struck through his flannel shirt and felt good.

"Glenn," he called.

A door with a pane of corrugated glass led from the front office into the shop at the rear, where the linotype and presses and other mechanical equipment were located. Through the door a monotonous, unobtrusive clicking had been audible; now it stopped, and a tall, thin man came into the office. His nose was long and red and pointed; he wore a red-and-white checked mackinaw and a woolen cap, pulled down over his ears; he was rubbing his hands together to warm them.

"Better thaw out a little," Brant said. "How's the stuff coming?"

Glenn Quarfield, printer, compositor and pressman, unbuttoned the mackinaw and fished a sack of tobacco out of his shirt pocket.

"Pretty good," he said, separating a thin leaf from a book of cigarette papers. "If the metal don't freeze in the pot we can roll the press before midnight."

The type metal couldn't freeze in the linotype pot, of course, but Brant's frown came back as he remembered that the electric current that melted it could be cut off if the storm brought down power lines.

"It's that cold out back, is it?"

"There's the pot, and an oil heater each side of me," Quarfield muttered, striking a match, "and I get up and swing my arms every five minutes. Thermometer on the wall says twenty above, but it's hell and gone colder'n that." He puffed his cigarette alight.

"The thermometer outside said twenty below the last time I looked," Carol volunteered. "I could almost see it shrinking."

Brant kicked the base of the stove. "These storms! It's always the same week or ten days of hell when a blizzard hits this country. No water except melted snow; no milk or fresh food; houses catching fire and all the mains frozen; people dying of exposure; wires down and no word from outside; fuel running low and everything stopped dead except snow shoveling."

His thoughts went on broodingly. Thirteen hundred people buried alive, sitting around waiting for it to be over, then laboriously digging themselves out. . . . Business at a standstill excepting in the saloons, where lumberjacks, millhands, fishermen and loafers drank cheap whiskey and fought gory fights. . . . A hodge-podge of Swedes, Poles, Finnlanders, French-Canadians, Scots and Irish, each breed hating all the others when they had nothing better to do than sit and hate. . . .

He remembered a newspaper clipping, months old, he had run across in Chuck Lyman's desk. He rummaged until he found it.

Quarfield was saying, "Might as well hold up the damn' paper. No sense going to press Thursday night if the streets are going to be closed Friday. Nobody'll get the paper on time. Half our readers may be dead, anyway—"

The front door burst open. An icy gust swept a cloud of glittering grains into the office and lumps of snow fell from the outer side of the door to the floor. A short, broad man came in, white as a ghost from head to foot.

"Shut it!" three voices chorused.

The newcomer put his back to the door and pushed. It closed with a crunching sound against the snow that had drifted into the doorway. The man looked at them out of mild blue eyes beneath brows that were tufted comically with white. He drew off a fur mitten and brushed his eyebrows. He unwrapped his muffler from a plump, weather-beaten face graven with stern but not unkindly lines.

"Quite a little flurry," he observed in a voice as mild as his eyes. "Bet you're glad to be back, Andy."

Brant nodded gravely. "Almost like it used to be when I was young, Sheriff."

Sheriff Ed Worth smiled. "It can keep on storming from now till doomsday for all of me. Storms are like vacations for peace officers. No auto accidents, no store burglaries, no calls out into the country."

"But plenty of barroom fights."

The sheriff used his fur hat to slap snow from his mackinaw, which was as long as an overcoat. He unhooked the collar and unbuttoned the front.

He said, "For me a barroom fight is as good as a rest any day."

Brant perched on the edge of the desk, smoothing the newspaper clipping between his fingers. "Ed, I'll bet you don't realize how many murderers and criminals there are in Red Rock. For days now they won't have anything to do but murder and commit crimes."

The sheriff was unperturbed. "I got the last murderer two years back. Remember when Indian Steve chopped off his partner's head with an ax? He's doing life in Marquette. One or two lumberjacks tried to fight with axes after that, but I whipped the daylights out of 'em and it kind of went out of fashion."

Worth's head came only a couple of inches above Brant's shoulders, yet Brant knew the other was not so much bragging about his fighting ability as stating an established fact. Worth had a pair of shoulders as wide as the door against which he leaned and a chest as big and deep as a

cider-barrel, and his short bow legs and long arms had the
strength of three ordinary men in them. Brant had seen
him squeeze and pound three ordinary men into insensi-
bility.

"You don't know people," said Brant, coaxing the argument along. "The way they are deep down inside, I mean."

"I know the ones around here that make trouble. Big
Al Nowka starts fights and bothers women when he's
liquored. The Wessendorf kids and young Dick Brinker
steal everything they can get their hands on, and busted
Jay Goldman's window last week. And there's old Maggie
Tucker that sells rotgut whiskey at her place and—"

"There are two murderers in Red Rock," Brant said,
"and I'll bet ten dollars you can't name either of them."

The sheriff stared. "Huh?"

"It says so right here." Brant held out the clipping.
"In any representative cross-section of the population, one
person in every thirty-seven will commit a crime and one
in every six hundred and fifty will commit murder. We
have thirteen hundred people—"

"Who said that?"

"The American Bar Association. It goes on to say that
the cost of crime is one hundred and fifteen dollars a year
for every man, woman and child. That makes Red Rock's
crime bill close to a hundred and fifty thousand."

"Hell." Worth snorted. "The whole population of Red
Rock County don't make that much in a year. If you want
the real story of what crime costs in these parts, I can give
it to you. My salary is sixteen hundred and fifty dollars,
which some folks think is too much. Ray Saunders, my
chief deputy, gets twelve-fifty. We get fifty cents a day for
keeping prisoners in the court house jail and last year it
came to just over two hundred dollars. Judge Thorpe, who
handles all criminal cases, is paid six hundred and fifty

salary and about the same in fees. Put down five hundred for traveling expenses and—"

"Skip it, Ed. We could add what it costs to keep Indian Steve in Marquette Prison for the rest of his life, and what Goldman lost when the Wessendorf kids and Dick Brinker broke his window, and the expense of keeping state troopers around, and what the state loses because Maggie Tucker hasn't any liquor license—but we won't bother. I'm interested in the murderers. They make the best news. Wonder which two citizens they are?"

Quarfield was rolling another cigarette, showing no disposition to return to the frigid atmosphere of the shop. He said, "Several of the boys are thinking of killing Ralston Crane, if he don't start paying some of the dough he lost playing poker at Gene Glebb's poolroom." Crane was the new assistant manager at the paper mill. "I'm one of the bloodthirstiest of 'em," Quarfield concluded, lighting his cigarette.

"A love murder would make better headlines," Carol put in. "I looked out the window and saw Crane walking past our house with Ella Macfarlane late last night. He had his arm around her and she had her head on his shoulder and looked as if she was crying." "Wait a minute," Brant said. "You can't mean Ella."

"Yes, I can. I'm not gossiping, either, if that's what you're getting at. It's just among us four, and I wouldn't go around spreading it for the world. I like Ella as well as anybody, even if I don't think she's a lily-white angel, like most of the men do—"

She stopped talking and looked at Brant.

"Oh, oh," she said. "Andy, I clean forgot."

Brant took his pipe from the desk and polished its bowl abstractedly with his thumb. "I'm a little surprised, that's all. John Macfarlane is a pretty good friend of mine and

I always did think Ella was all right." He spoke slowly to hide his inner disturbance. "Of course, there's probably a perfectly innocent explanation."

"Maybe," Quarfield suggested darkly, "it was Lola Tucker with him. She was out somewhere last night. She's about the same build as Ella, and Crane has been trying to get next to her for a long time."

Brant glanced at him sharply. It was well known in Red Rock that Quarfield considered himself invested with proprietary rights in Lola Tucker, the half-Indian waitress at the Northland Cafe, and had announced publicly in Sam Oliphant's saloon that he would thrash any man who tried to trespass.

Sheriff Worth buttoned his mackinaw and wrapped the muffler about his mouth and nose. His voice came dully.

"John Macfarlane has got one of the worst tempers I ever saw. Tried his doggonedest to kill a feller who said something about his first wife twelve years ago. Took four of us to hold him. I always did say he was a fool to get married again after Bertha died—and if he had to get married, why pick a girl half his age?"

He waved his arm vaguely, pulled his hat as low over his head as possible and opened the door. Pellets of snow spat against the stove and the wind came in with a vicious whine.

Brant stared at the closed door. "Whatever he stopped by for," he observed, "he forgot all about it. Ed's an absent-minded old coot." He managed a grin that was hardly a reflection of his feelings. Actually he was worried about John and Ella Macfarlane, who had influenced his life so profoundly and so differently.

John Macfarlane, the rugged, two-fisted fighter who had picked his line and battled his way to the head of it without asking aid or quarter from anyone, had found time all along the way to help the other fellow. Andrew had been in a military school in Wisconsin when a forest fire caught his mother and father in their summer cabin at Wapiti Lake, and after that

Macfarlane had devoted as much time to settling the affairs of the Brant Lumber Company and giving the boy a start in the world as he had to the running of his own Red Rock Paper Company. Mac was a grand man and a loyal friend—too grand and too loyal to be hurt, if Andy could prevent it.

And Mac was so deeply in love with the dark-haired girl who had come up from Grand Rapids to be his secretary that nothing short of tragedy could come from such an affair as Carol had hinted at. That knowledge had troubled Brant before this, but not because he had ever suspected that Ralston Crane was seeing too much of Ella.

Ella Morgan had been Brant's fiancée once. They had fallen in love when they were both students at Michigan State, and later it was Brant who had persuaded her to come to Red Rock to work for Macfarlane. But soon after her arrival Brant had gone away to learn the newspaper business, and as he became immersed in the problems of beginning his chosen career his visits and letters became few and far between.

He was awakened to the extent of his neglect and its consequences too late. Ella's last letter, telling him that she was going to be married to Macfarlane, had reached him a year ago. Since then Brant had known no peace when he thought of her, which was every day of his life.

"I guess I spoke out of turn." Carol shivered, not altogether because of the cold draft that had followed Worth's exit. "I didn't think. We were all friends, and anyway we women don't look at things the way you men do. I haven't the slightest doubt it was harmless enough."

Brant grinned at Carol and said scoffingly, "What's eating you, Scoop? It's a good thing you did mention it, because you reminded me of something I wanted to check on. There was a rumor around Oliphant's bar that Macfarlane was going to close the paper mill for the rest of the winter. That would put two hundred men on the town."

He lifted the receiver from the telephone on his desk and leaned toward the mouthpiece. When the operator came on he said, "Hi, Fanny, give me the paper mill." Then he said, "What do you make those wires of, anyway—spaghetti?" And hung up.

"Line down?" Quarfield inquired.

"Half the phones in town are out, and some of the trunk lines. The rest will go before morning. It's three blocks to the mill and I've got half an hour before the whistle blows." He pulled on overshoes that overlapped the cuffs of his trousers, wound a plaid muffler around his neck and face, shrugged into a mackinaw, donned a lumberjack cap with a flap that settled over his ears and thrust his hands into thick mittens.

"I'll get out the paper if we don't hear from you," Carol said. She had blocked out letters on a sheet of copy paper and she held it up for him to see. The letters formed a banner headline:

BRANT FEARED LOST IN STORM

"Save that," he told her. "Maybe you can use it. If I survive I'll meet you across the street for dinner."

It was a struggle pulling the door shut behind him, and then the wind took his breath away. Needlepoints of snow stung as much of his face as was exposed, so that he had to squeeze his eyes almost shut. It was only half-past four and darkness had not yet fallen, but it was impossible to see more than a few yards through the swirling white curtain.

2

No cars moved in Superior Street, the main business thoroughfare of Red Rock. The road and sidewalk were drifted over and in places the powdery snow came above Brant's knees. Before he had reached the first corner his face was stiff and aching and the cold seemed to penetrate his heavy clothing as if it were made of cheesecloth.

Near the end of the second block the tinny thump of a nickel-in-the-slot piano reached his ears above the noise of the gale. He squinted through ice-encrusted lashes and saw that he was in front of Joe Eckstrom's bar. He stumbled in, tired and winded, and leaned back against the door to close it.

Joe Eckstrom, the gray-mustached Swede, took one look at him and reached for the brandy bottle on the back bar. "I t'ink you don't want no water," he said.

"No water is right," Brant gasped. He filled a glass and drank it at a gulp. The brandy was cold as spring water going down, but it was warm in his stomach and the warmth spread.

Eckstrom's was a dismal place, with a scarred bar and splintery tables and dirty brown walls. There were a dozen men in working clothes, most of them from the Wessendorf sawmill, which closed for the day at four o'clock.

One dark-skinned little French-Canadian was from the paper mill, though, and he held the floor for the moment.

"So, by dam'," the French-Canadian was saying, "thees bas'ard Crane he fin' me an' Charlie King weeth a cigarette an' he say, 'By dam', you are both fire'.' So I say to hell, an' put on my coat an' go out. Charlie he say, 'I stay an' keel dat bas'ard.'" The man laughed. "He stay. By dam', maybe he keel heem, too!"

The heat of the cast-iron stove in the center of the room was beginning to soak into Brant's garments, but it was less intense than the heat of his thoughts as they dwelt on Ralston Crane. The new assistant manager of the mill lived at the Northland Hotel, across the street from the *Reporter* office, and Brant, who also stayed there, had met him two or three times without either liking or disliking him. From what he had heard, however, he judged that Crane was a misfit in this country of strong men who could be as rude and elemental as the blizzard outside. To begin with, he was a city man, with a smooth way of acting and talking that did not sit well with the workers over whom he was placed. He was in his thirties, and was graceful and handsome in a rather feminine way. He drank at all the bars, but did not hold his drinks well; while at Gene Glebb's poolroom, where poker games were held regularly, he had earned a reputation as an overbearing winner and a bad loser. Apparently Crane knew nothing about the tricky art of turning spruce logs into paper, which made it hard to understand why Macfarlane had brought him north two months ago to be general manager of the mill. And it was even harder for Brant to understand how a girl as fine as Ella could become interested enough in him to walk with him at night and weep upon his shoulder.

Swallowing a second drink, Brant placed some coins on the bar and buttoned up. He put his head down and plunged into the storm.

The five-o'clock whistle at the paper mill was like a siren, rising and falling on the gale, and before he reached the small stone building that contained the offices, men began to hustle past him in a long line, grotesquely bundled, each treading in the footsteps of the one ahead. They watched the snow at their feet and nothing else.

Brant went into the office building. While he caught his breath he looked at the plump blonde girl sitting on the bench in the reception room, buckling on overshoes. She was Dorothy Clay, the switchboard operator and receptionist.

"Hey, snow man," she greeted him. "I'll elope to Tahiti any time you say."

"Leave God's country, where red corpuscles are made?" He pretended to be shocked. "Where's Mac?"

"He went over to the mill half an hour ago. You can catch him there."

"Crane might do. Where's he?"

"I haven't seen him all afternoon."

He said, "I'll hunt them up. What do you know about the men being laid off?"

"Two of them were—Frenchie Lavoie and Charlie King. The new straw boss caught them smoking in the stockroom. King was waiting around to see Mac about getting his job back, but I guess he got tired."

"I mean a complete shutdown."

"There won't be any. We've got orders ahead, mister."

He went out. The rectangular brick building of the mill was entirely separated from the office unit, and as he stepped into the open space between them he was struck by the full force of the storm off the lake, sweeping across terrain that was bare of trees and houses. It all but knocked him off his feet, and for a moment he shrank back into the doorway.

As he huddled there he saw two figures emerge from a watchman's shack near the railroad spur and race for the door of the mill nearest the loading platform and farthest from him. Blurred as his vision was, he recognized the white-jacketed, white-capped form of Ella Macfarlane, while the man with her, in the fur-collared leather jacket and scarlet hunting cap, was Ralston Crane.

They disappeared into the mill, Crane in the lead. Ella was clinging to his arm, literally being dragged by him, unmistakably trying with all her slender might to hold him back. Brant felt his anger rising, but he made himself wait. Whatever was happening was strictly Ella's and Crane's affair, and perhaps Mac's. He had no right or reason to interfere.

He went to the nearest door of the mill and pulled it open. The deafening clatter of machinery greeted him and the aromatic smell of chopped spruce tingled in his nostrils. It was almost as cold inside the long building as it was outdoors, but there was no snow or driving wind. This side of the mill was partitioned off from the paper-making machine in the section Ella and Crane had entered. It was nearly dark; one yellow bulb glowed ahead of him, but its rays were feeble.

Brant peered right and left without seeing anyone. Beams, shafts and tanks would have hidden Macfarlane from his view, in any event, and the regular workmen could be counted on to leave the premises within five minutes of the whistle's signal. But there should have been someone around, for from one end of the place to the other wheels were turning, belts slapping and four-foot logs bumping along in a deep trough with a bottom of revolving rollers.

Sensing something extraordinary and ominous, Brant started at the end of the trough where the logs came up through the floor on an endless belt, stripped of bark and washed clean, and tumbled into the conveyor. He walked beside them, where men should have been standing with sharp steel hooks, watching for logs with knots and other blemishes, dragging them out to be sawn or shaved or thrown away. He walked fifty feet to the steel drum of the chopper, where the noise was loudest, and stood fascinated.

The drum was filled with spinning knives, visible through an opening into which the logs slid endwise. The flashing blades bit into the fibrous wood with a snarl, chewing it ravenously. Within ten seconds a twelve-inch-log, which had taken a man's lifetime to grow, became a flutter of half-inch chips which were sucked up through a square wooden flue to be bruised between iron rollers and dumped into a vast tank of churning yellow mush.

In this tank, called a digester, a mixture of lime, sulphuric acid and woodpulp was stirred by metal paddles while steam pipes heated it. For eighteen hours the mess would cook, bubbling sluggishly, before being pumped into the series of bleaching tanks, refiners and dyeing vats. Finally it would be thinned with clear water and started on its careful course through the long paper machine with its sand traps, wire cloth, suction boxes, felt cylinders, ironing rollers and surfacing calenders.

The log he watched slide into the bright knives this Thursday would, normally, be Red Rock bond paper in the stockroom Saturday afternoon.

The first time Brant had been in the mill, years ago, Mac had stopped him beside the cutting machine and said, "If ever you want anybody killed and don't want to go to prison for it, bring him here and we'll send him through."

"Perfect crime, eh?" Brant had asked.

There would be no possible way of proving the *corpus delicti,* according to Macfarlane. Chips from the logs that came after would polish the knives and obliterate blood-stains. Flesh, bones and clothing would be absorbed in the thousands of gallons of pulp and acid. Not even the most searching analysis would disclose the presence of human chemicals in that smelly sea.

"How about coins, buckles, shoe nails?" Brant had wondered.

"Try to find 'em. They'd be eliminated automatically. We get rid of tons of waste every day."

Remembering, Brant shuddered.

The chopper was at the end of the trough. At the other side of the machine, built into the partition, with doors facing either side of the mill, was the foreman's little room, in which was the switch that started and stopped the machinery. Crane and Ella, or Macfarlane—or all three of them—would be there, Brant thought.

He rounded the chopper and stopped short, staring at the floor. A scarlet hunting cap lay there, and a few inches from it was a fur-lined mitten, and he was sure they had been worn not ten minutes ago by Crane.

Brant's gaze traveled to the boarded sides of the conveyor and came to rest upon a long wet streak on the upper edge of one of the planks. He touched the streak and a sticky spot adhered to his mitten. Then all his horrified brain could think of was that he had to stop this murderous machine, even if it were too late to reclaim anything that had become a part of the bubbling acid mess in the digester.

He swung toward the open door of the foreman's room. He saw the switch handle protruding from its metal box just as his feet struck a man's body lying on the floor. Falling, he threw out an arm and hit the handle. The racket lessened immediately, the shriek of belted wheels became a groan, the thumping of the logs ceased. Before Brant could pick himself up the long building was still.

Crouched on hands and knees, Brant peered into the face of the man on the floor. The man was John Macfarlane. He lay on his back, his arms outflung, his round bearskin cap tumbled from his iron-gray hair. The flesh about his left eye was swelling redly and a blow of some kind had split his lip at one corner, spilling blood along the line of his jaw. But that same trickle of blood told Brant that Macfarlane still lived.

"Mac!" he yelled, gripping the big shoulders and shaking them. He lifted the man to a sitting position. "What happened, Mac?"

Macfarlane moaned. His eyes opened. They were slate-gray and the left one was shot with blood. He lifted a hand to the back of his skull.

"Hit my head," he whispered. "Must have fallen."

"You were knocked down, Mac. You've got a black eye and a split lip. Who did it?"

The paper manufacturer took a deep breath. He felt of his injured eye and the cut at the corner of his mouth. He began to swear huskily, calling upon a rich vocabulary acquired in fifty years spent among eloquently profane men.

"Crane," he said. "It was that damned double-crossing Crane. We were fighting and I must have slipped."

"Fighting?" Brant echoed. "Listen, Mac, was—was he alone?"

"Huh? Sure, he was alone. He didn't hurt me, I tell you—I slipped. I was going to kill the skunk and I still am." He started to get to his feet, none too steadily. "Where'd he go?"

Brant gulped. "It looks as if he went into the log conveyor. Into the conveyor and into those knives and—"

"*What?*"

"There was blood—" Brant began, and fell silent. A man had stepped around the end of the chopper. He wore blue denim coveralls, bulging with sweaters and trousers underneath. He was short and heavy and his battered nose slanted across his face like an unlucky prizefighter's. One side of his mouth was stretched in a lopsided smile.

"Charlie King," Brant said.

"Hyah, Andy." King's small eyes studied the marks of combat on the mill owner's face. "Mister Macfarlane, I been lookin' for you. You was the one that hired me, an' if I'm fired off this job after seven years, you're the one that's got to do it."

"Fired?" Macfarlane repeated. "Who said so?"

"The new straw boss, Crane."

Macfarlane's nostrils flared. "If that yellow-livered rat fired you—" He changed his mind about what he had been going to say. "Listen, King, I'm busy. Come around and see me tomorrow."

"I'll be here," King said. "I'll be here in time for work."

He walked away, favoring his right leg, which was stiff from an old fracture. Brant stared after the departing figure and his jaw tightened. "I wonder how long he was standing there listening," he said.

"Eh?" Macfarlane leaned against the edge of the door. "Give it to me straight, Andy. You said Crane went into the chopper. You said there was blood."

"Blood and his cap and one of his mittens." Brant turned, his arm outstretched to point. "But they're gone!"

A gust of cold wind reached them together with the noise of a door slamming.

3

Macfarlane grunted. "King took 'em. I saw him stuff something under his coat. What was the idea?"

"I can guess. Blackmail. Mac, are you sure Crane was
alone?"

"Of course he was. Who'd be with him? What are you
trying to get at?"

Brant shrugged. "Just trying to get it clear."

"Crane's around somewhere." Macfarlane sounded sure
of himself. "I don't know why he left his cap and mitt, but
he didn't go through that chopper. He couldn't have. I cut
off the power a minute or two before he showed up."

"The power was on when I came in, Mac. Every piece of
machinery in the place was going full blast. You were out
cold and I shut off the switch."

Macfarlane's eyes focused on Brant's face. His jaw hard-
ened till its hinges made lumps in his gray cheeks.

"No fooling, Andy?"

"No fooling."

"Then I reckon I must have killed him. God knows I'd
thought about it often enough."

So Macfarlane did know about Crane and Ella. The
discovery must have been a terrific shock to the older
man, whose love for his young and lovely second wife pro-
claimed itself in the inflection of his voice when he spoke

her name, in the glow in his eyes when he looked at her, in the gentleness with which he touched her arm when they walked together.

"We'll probably find Crane wandering around the place," Brant said hurriedly. "You probably hit him so hard he forgot his cap."

"No." Macfarlane was eyeing the wet streak on the conveyor.

"It might be your own blood."

"No, only my lip is bleeding, and it's just a trickle. It's broken, not torn, as it would be if it had scraped that plank."

"We'd better have a look, anyway."

"And after we've looked for a couple days, Andy, we can write our names across his face with a fountain pen." Macfarlane's lips were curved in a bitter smile. "You know, he was a skunk. I was doing my damnedest to make a man of him, but you can't make a man out of a skunk. He was trying to stab me in the back all along. He came to me today and made some tall demands. I might have let it pass, but he brought in someone else's name and I tried to break his rotten neck." Brant nodded, knowing whose name it had been, and wondering where Ella was now. "Crane can fight, for all his yellowness," Mac continued. "He handed me a couple that made me kind of lose touch."

"So you took a tumble and hit your head. You were out cold for ten minutes. How could you have killed him?"

"You don't know how mad I can get, Andy. Sometimes I can't remember anything afterward. I could have picked him up by the front of his coat, chucked him in the trough, turned on the machinery and then gone to sleep. I've been out on my feet and still fighting before this."

"It's a screwy notion, Mac. Forget it."

"It may be screwy, but I'll bet it's what happened."

"You're getting an obsession." Brant grasped Mac's elbow. "Come on and we'll have a look for Crane."

They went farther back into the mill, through a forest of criss-cross steel girders that supported mammoth tanks and boilers. Brant looked up at the bulging round bottoms of the digesters and wondered if there were chunks of flesh and bone and cloth mixed with the woodpulp, cooking in acid and lime.

They found Tony Brinker squinting at a gauge on a pipe elbow. Brinker was in sole charge of this part of the mill for the next eight hours, his job being to watch dials, adjust valves and make sure that nothing blew up or boiled over.

"Anybody been in since the gang quit?" asked Mac.

"I seen Charlie King," replied Brinker, his dark eyes unwinking in his round face. "He come down from the powerhouse and went toward the pulp room."

"How about Crane?"

Brinker spat a brown stream of tobacco juice toward a waste box. "Ain't seen him since I come on the job."

"No one else?" Brant inquired.

"No one else."

They went through another door and climbed skeletal steel stairways. The air warmed as they went higher. They emerged on a platform of metal bars built around the asbestos-covered tops of steam boilers, heated by furnaces force-fed with powdered coal. They faced a blackboard as high as a man and twenty feet long, studded with copper switches and gleaming dials.

Jim Scott, one of the engineers, sat in a chair tilted against the enameled casing of a humming generator. He had a magazine in his lap. He waved a gloved hand and said, "Hello."

"Where's Crane?" Macfarlane asked.

Tugging at his bristly mustache, Scott said he had not seen Crane and would not grieve if he never saw him again. "We got along quite a spell with just you as boss," he added, "and that's the way it ought to keep on being."

Brant asked, "Any visitors?"

"Charlie King was looking for Mac. Said Crane fired him. Said maybe he'd make Crane into pulp."

Brant started, but Macfarlane only smiled again. Mac said, "Come over to my office, Andy. I've got some Scotch."

They went down the steel stairs, past the chopper and the log conveyer and out across the open space, to the office building. Macfarlane did not pull the folds of the fur cap over his ears or button the collar of his jacket when he strode through the storm-hell. It was dark outside, as dark as it ever gets when the ground is white with snow, and the wind had increased. Macfarlane walked ahead, and his tracks were blotted out before Brant could step in them.

Macfarlane unlocked the door of the office and Brant followed him inside and made his teeth stop chattering. The older man switched on lights and they went into a large office in a corner of the building. The floor was carpeted, there were thick drapes at the windows, the valve of the steam radiator purred comfortably.

The bottle and glasses occupied the bottom drawer of a filing cabinet. Mac stood them on his desk blotter. He tossed his cap and mackinaw on a table and sat down in the cushioned chair behind the desk.

"You don't mind drinking with a murderer, Andy?"

"Cut it out," Brant pleaded. He picked up the bottle, poured whiskey into both glasses, got water from the lavatory and sat in a leather armchair. "If Crane's really dead, I think King killed him. He threatened to do it."

"He wouldn't have the guts."

"Why not? Supposing he was in the place, watching, while you and Crane were trading punches? When you went down and out, he could sneak up behind Crane and hit him with a log. Or maybe Crane saw him and picked a fight, and King slugged him, then dumped the body into the conveyor and turned on the juice. Everybody knows the best way to keep from being convicted of a murder, when there are no witnesses, is to make sure the body won't be found."

But that did not explain what had happened to Ella. . . .

"It doesn't sound right," Macfarlane objected.

"It sounds right to me. Probably I came in just as King was finishing up, and he hid behind something. He didn't have time to pick up Crane's cap and mitt. He stayed out of sight for a while and then pretended he'd just come in from somewhere else."

"Maybe. On the other hand, I'm not going to kid myself. When I go up in front of the Almighty with a list of sins as long as my life to answer for, I don't want to seem to be trying to lie out of any of them. Between the two of us, I'll take the blame for this."

"Meaning you want to think you did it?"

Macfarlane drank his whiskey and took a cigar out of a box on the desk. "Meaning I don't give a damn. My conscience won't bother me. As far as the law is concerned, Ed Worth would have a hell of a time proving Crane is dead, and so would the state police. I'll make fine bond paper out of Crane after I bleach the yellow out of the pulp. I'll make you a present of some of it."

"You're giving me jitters," Brant said. "I'm not as tough as you."

"You're tough enough to keep this to yourself, aren't you?"

Brant looked him in the eye. "You know I am. You and I have been friends for a long time. You can bump off anybody you like, and I'll swear it was two other fellows."

Macfarlane bit the end from the cigar and struck a match. "I wouldn't care who knew it, except for Ella. If

I didn't think it would hurt her, I'd go around bragging about killing Crane and daring them to do something." He puffed clouds of blue smoke and his eyes softened. "But I don't want Ella worried, Andy. She wouldn't understand. I wouldn't for a minute have her think there was blood on my hands, even skunk blood. So Ella and everybody else can just think Crane wandered out into the blizzard and froze to death. It's happened before this to a lot of men and some of their bodies have never been found."

His eyes went hard again, glinting like polished spear-points. "Andy, I'm the sort of guy who could kill a man every day in the week if I thought I was justified. I'd kill anybody who tried to make trouble that would react on Ella. I'm thinking about Charlie King. Maybe he didn't see or hear anything—but if he did, and if he's got ideas about blackmail, he'd better watch his step."

Brant envied the rugged self-sufficiency of the man. "I'm with you all the way, Mac," he said, "but there's no sense in looking for trouble. The thing's over and done with, however it was. Let's get out of here."

"I've got to stick around. We'll probably have to shut down for the storm, and I'll have to make arrangements. Stop and tell Ella I'll be late for supper, will you?"

"Why don't you—?"

"Damn it, how can I phone with the lines down? Don't tell me you're scared of my wife, Andy, after being her schoolboy sweetheart. Just say I may be two or three hours, and if supper's ready you're to eat my share."

John and Ella Macfarlane lived in a square brick house, more nearly a mansion than any other in Red Rock, half a block from Superior Street in Alger Avenue. It was only about as far from the mill as it was from Eckstrom's bar to the mill, but Brant found the wind fiercer than when he had left his office an hour before. The mere act of walking was an exertion that overtaxed lungs and muscles, and he reeled with fatigue as he crossed the crunching carpet of snow on the porch, opened the storm door and pressed the bell button. Ella was an indistinct blur before his streaming eyes, as she greeted him.

"Andy, come in this minute, snow and all. Never mind the rugs. Mac isn't home yet, but he will be."

Steam radiators and a cheerful blaze of logs in the stone fireplace filled the living room with aggressive warmth. Brant unbuttoned his coat and wiped the melting ice from his face with a handkerchief, feeling oddly embarrassed.

"Mac asked me to stop by. He'll be at the office two or three hours, changing work schedules."

Ella helped him out of the mackinaw. "Sit down and get warm, anyway. I'm sorry about Mac; I was wishing he'd hurry. It isn't nice, being alone on a night like this." A hint of anxiety crept into her tone. "There isn't . . . any trouble?"

He stood with his back to the fire. The shifting light of the flames was all that relieved the dusk of the long room, with its solid chairs and bearskin rug and the antlered elk's head on the farther wall. Ella hung his mackinaw on the rack near the stairway.

"Trouble?" He watched her closely. "Everything was peaceful when I left. Mac was alone."

She came toward him, her eyes flecked with golden grains of light. "Wasn't . . . Ralston Crane there?"

Her dark hair was wound like a scarf about her small head. Her oval face with its arched brows and grave mouth reminded him of an ivory carving he had seen in a museum. Her body was so youthfully alive that he was aware of its every curve beneath her brown skirt and yellow blouse.

He shook his head. "I looked for Crane. He wasn't in sight."

"Oh." He thought he detected relief and a faint puzzlement in her manner as she sank into a low chair, crossing slim legs that were daintier in ribbed wool than most in gossamer silk.

What could a girl like Ella have in common with a person like Crane? Why had she been with him in that watchman's shack, and from what purpose had she been trying to restrain him? Above all, where had she been when Macfarlane and Crane fought, and later?

She took an enameled box from a table, selected a cigarette and offered one to Brant. He declined it, found a packet of matches in his pocket and struck one for her. Dark lashes veiled her eyes as she leaned toward the flame.

"How was Mac, Andy? Did he seem . . . worried?"

"He seemed tired. He'd hurt his eye some way around the mill, running into something or falling."

She made a quick movement. "I'd better go to him."

"No," Brant said. "He wouldn't want you out in this weather. He's all right; he was feeling fine when I left. He'll be sore because I told you he was hurt. He'd go a long way to keep from upsetting you."

"Yes." She exhaled smoke slowly. "He'd go a long way. He's grand, Andy—one of the grandest men I've ever known. I'd go just as far to keep from making trouble for him, if I knew how . . . but instead, I've hurt him a lot."

"Hurt him?" Brant was incredulous. "You've made him happier than he ever was. He worships the ground you walk on."

"That makes it harder." She crushed out the cigarette, although it had hardly begun to burn. "Sometimes I wish we hadn't been married. It sounds like a disloyal thing to say, but I don't mean to be disloyal and I wouldn't say it to anyone but you, because you like him, too. I love him, Andy—I really do—and yet I can't help thinking he'd be better off without me."

He understood nothing clearly except that she was wholly sincere and there were tears in her eyes. He sat on the footstool beside her chair and took the nearer of her hands in both of his.

He said, "Ella, the two people I care about above all others are you and Mac. Isn't there some way I can help?"

She shook her head, smiling a little. "If there was, I wouldn't hesitate to ask it."

"Is it that you're personally unhappy?"

"If that were all, I wouldn't give it a second thought. If I regretted my bargain in marrying him, I'd still keep it without whining. As it happens, I don't regret it; I respect Mac and honor him, and if it weren't for one other person I'd be as happy with him as anyone had a right to expect to be."

"Is Crane that other person?" It was a hard question, but he had to ask it.

She was silent. Brant asked another question.

"Ella, you—you're not . . . involved with that—with him?"

She stared in amazement. "Involved with Ralston? You mean . . . that way? Andy Brant, that's the most ridiculous thing I ever heard you say. I love Mac, and I'm afraid I love you a little—just enough so that it hurts sometimes—and between the two of you all my love is taken up. I despise Ralston, but . . ."

"But what?"

"Nothing. I'd trust you with any secret that was mine, but don't ask me what concerns anyone else."

"Would it help if I should break his neck?"

"Oh, no. Promise you won't try."

He had forgotten for the moment that it was doubtful whether Crane still had a neck that could be broken.

"It's a promise."

"You'd do just about anything I asked, wouldn't you?"

"Anything, Ella."

Their eyes met, and between them arose an understanding that was somehow more intimate than an embrace could ever be. There was an ache in his throat and his fingers tightened around her hand. . . .

The clock on the mantel whirred a warning. A tiny gong struck six times.

Brant stood up hastily. "I'm late."

"You can't stay for . . . for dinner?"

"This is my busy night. I shouldn't."

Her arm trembled, reaching for the cigarette box again. "It was nice of you to drop in."

Turning up his coat collar, he paused with his hand on the doorknob and looked at her, sitting motionless in the moving firelight.

"Don't worry, Ella. You have two men to fight for you, and you can count on both of them no matter what happens."

"I'm a proud woman because of that," she said.

4

Eric Nordquist, proprietor of the Northland Hotel, lounged in a wicker chair in the lobby. His feet, shod in fleece-lined moccasins, were hoisted comfortably upon the cast-iron fender of the fat base-burner; his head, covered with straight white hair that appeared to sprout from the top center of his skull and radiate downward in all directions like the grass roof of a Fiji Islander's hut, was propped upon a cushion stuffed with fragrant balsam needles; his gaunt face supported a gray stubble of beard and a maze of deep lines grooved by many Upper Peninsula winters, and his huge hands, clasped upon his chest, were remarkable for the fact that the two middle fingers of each were webbed together.

When Brant came into the lobby, letting in a little of the mounting fury of the blizzard, Nordquist stopped talking to a pudgy man who occupied another wicker chair beside him. His faded blue eyes blinked.

"How cold?" he asked.

"Twenty-five below by your thermometer," Brant told him. "It's protected from the wind, there in the doorway, or the mercury would be down farther."

"You see?" Nordquist said to the pudgy man. "It's almost mild. I mind one winter thirty-two years ago—"

"Before you start on one of those yarns," Brant broke in, "tell me whether you've seen Ralston Crane."

"He ain't come in from the mill yet. This man is waiting for him. He come all the way from Detroit just to see Crane, so you ought to put a piece in the paper about it. His name is Rigby."

"Sure." Brant glanced at the pudgy man, who wore a soft black hat, a dark business suit and low shoes. The man's face was flabby and his round eyes were colorless. "You came on the afternoon train?"

Rigby grunted affirmatively.

"Well, there won't be any more trains for a while, so you're practically a resident. Mind telling me your full name and business?"

Rigby puffed out his cheeks. "I don't want nothing in the paper. My business is positively confidential. It's bad enough having to stay in a burg like this up near the North Pole without getting my name in the paper."

Brant raised his eyebrows. "Have it your own way. You aren't the only news this week. Better stay indoors with those clothes, though, or we'll be writing you up in the obituary column."

On his way to the door at the side of the lobby that led into the Northland Cafe, Brant paused at the desk long enough to look at the register. The man had signed himself "Peter Rigby, Detroit," in a tight, angular script, and had been given a room on the second floor, three doors from Brant's own.

Carol was in one of the mahogany-veneer booths in the cafe, eating apple pie, while Lola Tucker, the half-Indian waitress, gathered dishes from the porcelain-topped table.

"It's about time," Carol said. "I was going to tie a keg of brandy to a Saint Bernard and send it out to look for you."

"If you had, I'd be sleeping it off at the bottom of a drift. Hey, Lola, how about a steak this thick?"

Lola said, "Okay, Andy," in a tone of profound boredom. Her hair and eyes were jet black and her cream-colored face, with its high cheekbones, was strikingly pretty. Her body was supple and full of graceful curves that showed through her blue uniform smock. She had been married to a man who had deserted her, and now she lived in an old house on Mill Avenue with her full-blooded Iroquois mother, Maggie Tucker, who sold moonshine to millhands and lumberjacks and frequently entertained them at parties that lasted till dawn. It was generally conceded that Lola's moral code was no stricter than might have been expected—that several of her lengthy succession of sweethearts, of which Quarfield was avowedly determined to be the last, had found her none too constant—but few of the Northland's customers minded that.

Carol finished her pie and leaned back, patting her stomach indelicately. "I took a room here," she told Brant. "An inside room. I told my folks about it before the phone went."

"The *Reporter* will foot your hotel bill," he said. He was glad, for Carol lived with her family on the lakeshore, nearly a mile away, and it would be a bitter and dangerous walk tonight. "There'll be lots to do in the morning, and even if you managed to get home you probably wouldn't be able to get back."

"We don't go to press tonight, then?"

"What's the use? It will be afternoon before the snowplows can get the streets open, if they manage to do it at all. A lot of things will happen during the night. We'll hear of people who may be stranded in cars on the highway. We'll know how badly communications are disrupted. There'll be radio news from Detroit and Milwaukee and the *Mining Journal* station in Marquette—news of Washington and international doings—and we'll print as much as we can of that, since no outside papers will come in."

"We'll cover the world, huh?"

"You bet. We'll make up most of the paper tonight and save half the front page for the storm story and outside news. We'll go to press as soon as we can distribute papers. After that, as long as Red Rock is snowed under, we'll get out a daily bulletin on the job press."

"It sounds like fun."

"Fun, nothing. It will mean work and it will cost money we won't get back in a hurry. It will be unselfish public service—something all newspapers talk about, but few go in for."

Lola brought the steak. It was neither thick nor tender, but Brant ate it without complaint. He called for coffee and filled and lighted his pipe.

"Even in an inside room, it will be cold upstairs," he observed.

Carol pursed her lips in mock severity. "I may be a poor working girl, but I have my pride and my old-fashioned notions of what is proper for young ladies. No doubt you learned a lot of wickedness in the big cities, but—"

He blew smoke in her face. "I was going to say, I have an electric heater which I'll be glad to lend you. If the power lines hold out, it will be a help."

Her expression changed to one of reproach. "Every time I get a romantic idea you become ultrapractical. For two weeks I've been dreaming you'd insult me one day, and all you do is act polite and thoughtful."

Brant frowned. "Your folks were too easy with you when you were a little brat. You never got spanked."

"I did."

"Not hard enough or often enough." He finished his coffee and got up. "We'd better start back to work. I'm a romanticist at heart. Once I get started there's no stopping me."

"But you don't get started," she complained.

He helped her into her jacket. It was a garment of blue with a wide white stripe around the middle, made from one of those fleece-soft, iron-tough blankets imported into Canada from England by the Hudson Bay Company. She wore the trousers of a crimson ski suit over her skirt. When she put on her woolen scarf and gloves and pulled her blue woolen cap over her hair she looked like a slim, handsome boy.

Brant paid the check at the counter. He said, "Come on, Scoop," and took her arm and hustled her through the front door. They floundered through waist-deep drifts that filled the middle of Superior Street, and reached the office panting.

Quarfield was hugging the stove. "Everything's up but the storm story," he said. "Better get it out before the current goes."

"I'll give you the tail end of it," Brant decided. "We'll set up the lead two columns wide in the morning. If the machine quits we'll set it by hand in fourteen, twelve and ten-point. We'll handset late bulletins, too."

He pounded the typewriter furiously, while Carol sorted out society and personal paragraphs. Quarfield began to assemble the eight pages the *Reporter* would carry the next day. The three of them worked till nearly ten and had all but the last two forms made up when, abruptly, the lights went out.

"Quitting time," Brant said. He struck a match and led the way into the office, where the stove gave forth a dull red glow. He took an oil lamp from a shelf.

"Just like when grandma was a girl," said Carol.

Brant got the lamp burning. Its soft, yellowish light was not unpleasant.

"That's the way it goes," he murmured. "We brag about how civilized we are, with all our gadgets—nothing to do but press a button for light, heat and radio reception—

and then a little storm comes along and slaps us back fifty years. Yesterday we were a part of Michigan and of the United States; now Washington is as far away as Venus and the capitol at Lansing as far as the moon—"

"Venus," Quarfield said. "Now you're talking."

"If I had it in for somebody in this town," Brant went on, "I'd pick the next couple days to do him in. A murderer couldn't ask for a better break. He could—"

"Stop it!" cried Carol. "You're giving me the willies."

Brant had given himself the willies. He had not meant to say that. For the moment he had forgotten about John Macfarlane and Ralston Crane; his subconscious mind had remembered and had shaped his thoughts. "We'll take care of the storm lead and the headlines tomorrow morning," he said, changing his tone. "We'll turn the *Reporter* into a real newspaper for once. Who's going to have coffee?"

"Me," said Quarfield. "I'll break trail for you." He dropped the disintegrating stub of his cigarette into the coal scuttle, pulled his cap down over his ears, opened the door and squeezed through it.

Carol toyed with a sheet of paper upon her desk. "I guess we won't need this," she said. It was the paper upon which she had penciled the headline:

BRANT FEARED LOST IN STORM

"We'll use it," Brant said. "It will be the first eight-column line of your newspaper career. We won't change anything except the name."

He took the sheet from her and a heavy-leaded pencil from his breast pocket and altered the first and last letters of the name. The "B" became a "C," the "T" an "E."

"Crane," she said blankly.

He inclined his head.

"But how do you know he isn't at the hotel?"

"I asked before I met you in the restaurant."

"My goodness, give the man time—"

Something in his eyes silenced her. She had been perched on the edge of the desk. She slid off and reached for her jacket.

"I'm scared, Andy."

"No reason to be."

"But just this afternoon I said there might be a murder—"

"I started that murder talk. It was a bad subject. We'll steer away from it till there really is a murder, or anyway till the storm's over. About Crane, maybe he stopped somewhere for a drink or to play poker. Maybe he's got a girl friend between the paper mill and the hotel. We'll wait till morning before we set up that headline in ninety-six point."

The street lamps were out and the only lights in sight were from oil wicks and gasoline lanterns in the Northland and in Oliphant's bar. Quarfield's trail was not to be seen. Brant and Carol skirted a drift and entered the lobby of the hotel.

Peter Rigby was sitting in the same wicker chair, gnawing a toothpick gloomily.

"No luck?" Brant asked.

"I think he ducked town."

Brant said cheerfully, "He couldn't get far. Why not try the saloons?"

"Tried them already," Rigby growled.

The cafe was deserted except for Quarfield and Sleepless Sam, the night man. When they were seated in a booth Carol inquired, "Who's the sour-faced stranger?"

"Man of mystery. Calls himself Rigby, and he's waiting for Crane for reasons known only to himself. Might be a cop."

"He'll wait a long time," Quarfield prophesied. "Crane is the sort of guy who could smell a cop a mile."

They did little talking. The lights flickered and threw squirming shadows on the walls, and the monotonous sound of the wind gave them chills that had nothing to do with the temperature. Brant was surprised at his hangover of weariness from his brief bouts with the blizzard. He yawned over his coffee.

"Good night, all," Carol said, getting up. "Andy, I have room two-eleven, right across from you. If you hear me yell, come on the run. Remember, if you hear me yell."

"Good night, Scoop," he said.

A few minutes later he went up the creaking stairs to his own room, which adjoined Crane's. Before going in he tapped experimentally at Crane's door. All he could hear beyond it was a window pane rattling in the gale.

It was freezing cold in Brant's room. He groped in a bureau drawer for his flashlight and undressed swiftly within its circle of brilliance. He donned flannel pajamas, crawled between sheets that could not have been much warmer than a snowbank, wadded the blankets about himself and lay with chattering teeth.

Even after his body had driven the iciness from the sheets, he did not drop off to sleep right away. The weariness that had possessed him earlier had departed, and his brain churned with troublesome thoughts and ugly speculations.

He seemed to see the bright knives spinning in the log chopper at the paper mill, and to hear Macfarlane's voice rumbling, *"I'll make fine bond paper out of Crane after I bleach the yellow out of the pulp."* The sulphurous smell of the great cooking vats crept back into his nostrils. . . . Then he was looking into Ella's golden eyes, seeing visions there, feeling himself drawn to her as an iron toward a magnet—and afraid and ashamed of that feeling. . . . And the image of Carol came between them, and she was say-ing, *"A love murder would make better headlines. I looked out the window and saw Crane walking past our house with Ella Macfarlane last night. He had his arm around her and she had her head on his shoulder and looked as if she was crying."*

He thought about Charlie King's liberal threats to kill Crane. He wondered why Peter Rigby had traveled hun-dreds of miles to see Crane, arriving with that hard, fishy look in his colorless eyes just at the time Crane had van-ished so abruptly. Even when his body finally slept, his mind kept turning ceaselessly with dream-distorted recol-lections of the events of the day. Ella struggling to hold Crane back—splashes of bright blood against rough plank-ing—a soft and persistent knocking noise—

But there was nothing imaginary about the knocking. Brant continued to hear it after he had opened his eyes. He called irritably, "Who's there?" and heard above the storm sounds someone panting hoarsely outside the door, someone fumbling with the knob.

The cold lapped around him like water as he got out of bed. He felt on the top of the bureau for the flashlight, but did not find it.

The door creaked and opened. A gray shadow swayed against the blackness of the wall. His eyes could see noth-ing distinctly, but a breath of familiar perfume reached him, bringing instant recognition.

"Ella!"

He caught her in his arms as she leaned toward him. Her head sagged upon his shoulder; melted snow from her garments slid over his flesh inside his pajamas; his senses sharpened with the knowledge that something was terribly wrong.

"What happened, Ella?" he whispered fiercely, shaking her. "Stop being afraid and tell me."

Her breasts shuddered through her white jacket with the agony of her breathing.

"Oh, Andy! It's Mac . . . shot and dying . . . in his office at the mill. Andy, for God's sake, hurry—*hurry!*"

5

For an instant Brant suspected that he was dreaming still, and Ella with her shocking news was only a part of his nightmare. Then the reality of her terror gripped him.

"Sit down," he said, pushing her gently toward the bed. "Get your wind back and tell me about it. I'll be ready to go right away."

He retreated into the darkness, tore off his pajamas and groped for his clothes. The girl was a small shapeless blob huddled against his pillows; her breath was labored, and except for it there was no sound for half a minute.

She said finally, "He was on the floor. There was blood all over his chest. I got him on the sofa, but he wouldn't let me do anything. He said to get you."

"He didn't mention how it happened?"

"Just that it was an accident. It was hard for him to talk. Oh, Andy, I don't believe it! He was always so careful with guns."

"Accidents occur, just the same." He would have staked all he had that Mac had not shot himself, but it would never do to tell her so. "How did you happen to find him?"

"It was getting late—after eleven—and I couldn't think what might be keeping him. Thank God I went to see. I don't know how long he's been lying there."

The luminous dial of his wrist watch told Brant that it was twelve-thirty. He buckled his overshoes, buttoned his coat and found the flashlight where it had rolled to the edge of the bureau top.

"I'll go to the mill," he said. "You wake Doc Sperry and tell him to hustle there as fast as he can. Wait with Sperry's wife till we come back."

"I want to go with you."

"Don't be an idiot. You'd be in the way. We'll bring him straight to your house. Tony Brinker and Jim Scott are at the mill and they'll help."

They left the room together. In the hallway she stumbled and he put his arm around her waist.

"I don't know what I'd do without you," she said.

It seemed a senseless thing to say when both of them knew they were going to have to do without each other all their lives. Unless, he thought, this was really the end for John Macfarlane.

The snow was mounded four feet deep in front of the Northland, but Doctor Frank Sperry lived just across the corner and Brant knew she could get that far. He squeezed her shoulder.

"You'll have to make a lot of noise to wake him. Tell him it's a matter of life and death. And don't forget—wait there till I come for you."

He lowered his head against the wind and began the bitter journey toward the paper mill. It was like walking along the floor of an icy lake, sinking to his hips in ooze at every step. There would be stories in the papers in the next few days about farmers who had died between their barns and houses, motorists who had frozen in their cars, children who had lost their ways and would never return home.

Passing Oliphant's bar he heard laughter and saw the smoky flicker of lanterns. Oliphant's present customers, most of them, would remain where they were for the duration, and Brant did not blame them much.

The idea of Mac bleeding on the sofa in his office, possibly dying or already dead, kept his legs driving steadily when it seemed that his breath was exhausted and his lungs no longer capable of functioning. No one on earth was closer to him than the grizzled mill owner. If Mac died, Brant would feel the same bottomless sorrow he had felt at the loss of his parents.

Whatever had happened to Mac, no accident of his own making had sent that bullet into his chest; Brant was completely sure of that without quite understanding why—as sure as he was that no matter how it had been, Mac would lie to Ella to spare her. Nor could he make himself believe that Mac had shot himself deliberately after fifty-odd years of not being afraid of man or God.

Perhaps they had not searched well enough for Ralston Crane that afternoon. . . .

The front door of the stone office building was unlocked. Brant lunged through it, marveling that Ella could have made the trip. The feeble glow of an oil lamp marked the partly opened door of Mac's office, but it was dark in the reception room and he reached in his pocket with stiff fingers for the flashlight. In the cone of light he saw against the gray linoleum of the floor two separate trails of blood, thick splashes of it close together, between the inner office and the outer door.

Macfarlane lay on the leather couch beside his desk, his eyes closed, his hands holding a crimson towel to his left shoulder. His coat and vest were open and his shirt and undershirt partly unbuttoned, showing the hair of his chest matted with blood. He lay so still that Brant feared he was dead.

He laid his hand upon the pale forehead. "Mac," he said softly. "It's Andy."

The waxen eyelids moved and the lips whispered, "Andy?"

He bent over the sofa. "Take it easy, old timer. Doc Sperry's on the way. We'll have you fixed up in no time."

"Where's Ella?"

"She's all right. I told her to wait with Agnes Sperry till we got you home."

"Give me some whiskey, Andy."

He got the bottle of Scotch out of the filing drawer, covered the bottom of a tumbler with liquor and spilled in two inches of water, on the theory that a little whiskey would go a long way with a man in Mac's condition.

With Brant's help Mac raised his head, and if the movement caused him pain he gave no sign of it. When the rim of the glass clicked against his teeth he swallowed thirstily.

"What kind of a drink is that?" he protested.

"It'll do for a starter. Lie still and you'll begin to feel it."

Brant glanced around the room. There was an irregular puddle of blood where Mac must have lain until Ella found him. A large revolver lay on the floor in front of the desk and not far away the rug was rumpled and a chair was overturned. The smooth surface of the desk was marred by a deep groove, six inches long, unquestionably made by a bullet; behind the desk, on a line with the groove, there was an irregular white scar in the painted plaster of the wall, with a neat round hole in its center.

Mac was watching him. He spoke, no longer whispering, in a voice that was almost normal. "Straighten things up, will you, Andy?"

"Sure." He put the chair on its feet and stretched the rug smooth with his heel. He picked up the revolver, threw out the cylinder and saw that two of its six .38 caliber cartridges had been fired; he rubbed it with his hands, obliterating whatever fingerprints might have been on it, and placed it on the desk. He laid a copy of the Red Rock

County telephone directory over the groove in the desk and pushed Mac's swivel chair against the wall, where its back hid the hole in the plaster.

"All evidence destroyed," he reported.

"That's the idea." Mac closed his eyes again. "What did Ella tell you? Did she believe it was an accident?"

"Not entirely. She remembered you were always careful with guns."

"I wasn't careful enough with that one. You won't spoil my story?"

"Certainly not. Who did it? Not Crane?"

"Crane's in the pulp vat. It was Charlie King."

"Why, that double-crossing heel!"

"He was drunk, Andy. He came in, full of booze, and said he saw me throw Crane in the log chopper. He wanted five thousand dollars as a starter. I took the gun out of my desk to scare him, and the crazy fool grabbed for it. There were two shots, and the first thing I knew I was sitting in the corner and he was on his way out. . . . Give me another drink."

Brant mixed whiskey and water again and held the glass for Mac. "He got away?"

"I got up and chased him as far as the door. Then I had to quit because I knew I was caving in. I just made it back to the office. I was on the floor when Ella showed up."

"I'll take care of King for you."

"No, you won't. You'll keep your mouth shut and so will he—for nothing."

"But listen—"

"You listen to me, damn you! If he gets in trouble he'll tell about Crane. Otherwise he'll be scared to talk. If I get over this I'll take care of him in my own way. If I don't— well, sending King to prison won't help me. You let him know he's safe as long as he keeps his lip buttoned, but the minute he starts blabbing he'll be up against a murder charge, with you as chief witness against him."

It didn't seem fair. "Ella wouldn't want it that way."

"You idiot!" Mac's voice rose, gathering volume. "What Ella wants and what's good for her are two different things this time. It's bad enough having her worry about me getting shot without making her hate someone and be scared and bitter and—"

"Easy," Brant cautioned, alarmed at the wounded man's vehemence. "You're right, Mac. I see it now. You won't have to worry about me. Anyway, you're not going to die—not when you can yell that loud. Not if you save your strength."

Mac relaxed. "I'm trusting you."

"You know you can." He heard the outer door open. "Here's Doc now."

"Remember—I was fooling with the gun and it went off."

"I'm with you a hundred per cent. Sit tight." He turned toward the reception room. "In here, Doc! He's lost a lot of blood and—"

He stopped in astonishment, seeing that Sperry was not alone. Two figures tottered across the room, one sagging heavily against the other.

Sperry croaked, "Somebody take this fool woman off my hands! I had to lug her most of the way."

Brant hurried forward and grasped Ella. She was a dead weight in his arms and he lifted her as he would have lifted a child. She said faintly, "Don't bother—about me. I'm—all right. How is he?"

Through the layers of clothing they both wore he could feel her heart racing and pounding. He said angrily, "If you had done as you were told . . ." But pity came to him and he said, "If you were half as tough as you think you are . . ." Then he smiled and tightened his embrace. "You're all right, all right, and so is Mac. He's not going to die."

He carried her into the office, put her in a chair, un-buttoned her jacket and pulled off her mittens and began to rub her wrists.

Mac stared. "What's the matter with her, Andy?"

"Shut up!" Sperry commanded waspishly. "Nothing's the matter with her, except she didn't have sense enough to wait for us to bring you back. She had to come along and she couldn't make it under her own power. I brought my kid's toboggan for you and she rode on it, and I damn' near didn't make it myself."

The doctor had his coat and hat off. He was a small wiry man in his forties with a bald head and horn-rimmed spectacles and a perpetually harassed expression. He sawed away part of Mac's shirt and undershirt with a penknife, removed the blood-soaked towel and looked glumly at the wound.

"How long ago?"

"A little after eleven. I was getting ready to go home."

"Who did it?"

"Nobody. The gun was in my desk. I was checking it over and it went off."

Sperry snorted. "And you a grown man! An inch to the right and you'd be in a warmer climate this minute. You've lost a barrel of blood, but I guess you'll pull through if you stay in bed and follow orders."

"Thank God!" Ella said. Tears were streaming from her eyes. Brant was holding both her hands; he dropped them and began searching his pockets for a clean handkerchief.

"I'm going to get rough with you before I take you for a sleigh ride," said Sperry. "Think you can stand it?"

"Give me a drink and I can stand anything."

Brant said, "He had a couple of little ones."

"Hell, give him a big one. Give him the whole bottle if he wants it. He might as well be drunk as the way he is.

If a gun can't kill him, whiskey can't. I've got to go after the bullet and swab out that hole, and it's going to hurt."

It did hurt. Brant winced, seeing the spasms of pain cross Mac's face and the blood run from his bitten lips. Braced against the desk, the young man felt sweat break out on his forehead and had to keep swallowing against a sickish sensation in the pit of his stomach. Once more he wondered at Ella's strength and courage, watching her handle the blood-soaked cloths as the slow probing for the bullet progressed. She was white as death itself, but not once did she falter.

"Got it!" Sperry exclaimed finally, dropping a hard object on the floor beside the sofa and wiping the long forceps. "It was right smack against the shoulder blade. Wonder it didn't go clear through."

Then the swabbing with iodine and the packing and dressing. . . . Mac had four drinks before it was finished, all big ones, but they had no visible effect upon him.

"Reminds me of the time I had to amputate a leg in the woods near Au Train," Sperry said, washing his hands at the lavatory. "He was a young lumberjack and got caught under a falling tree. Took the better part of a gallon of whiskey to finish the job, but he didn't get drunk."

Brant went to the mill, borrowed Jim Scott's overcoat and got Tony Brinker to help. They brought the toboggan into the office and used it as a stretcher. Wrapped in his own coat and Scott's, Mac was carried outside. He lay perfectly still, saying nothing, his great strength nearly gone.

They had the storm at their backs during the short trip to the Macfarlane house. With Brinker to haul the toboggan, leaving Brant free to help Ella and Sperry to follow behind in the broken trail, they made it in fifteen minutes.

Half an hour later they had Mac undressed and in a bed brought from upstairs and placed in the dining room. The double doors between the living room and dining room were open and yellow flames licked around fat logs in the fireplace.

Sperry gave Mac a hypodermic injection. "That'll keep you quiet for a few hours, you old buzzard," he said. "You've made enough trouble for one night."

Brant had left his pipe at the hotel. He found a box of Mac's cigars and lit one when Sperry and Brinker had gone. Sitting in a big chair in front of the fire, he puffed drowsily.

"Coffee, Andy?" Ella asked.

"No. You get some sleep before you pass out. I'll be awake in case he needs me."

"Andy—" She came close and spoke softly. "Andy, it wasn't an accident, was it?"

"Good Lord, why not? Things like that happen every day. Why would he say it was an accident if it wasn't?"

"He's hiding something from me. You're both hiding something from me."

"Nonsense! You've had a bad night and your imagination is taking advantage of you. Lie down and you'll see things differently when you wake up."

"How about you?" Ella asked uncertainly.

"I'm going to sit here. I'm not a bit sleepy. If I catch myself dozing off, I'll wake you."

"All right," she consented unwillingly.

6

The smell of boiling coffee and frying bacon awoke Brant. He stirred and was surprised to find himself still in the chair in front of the fireplace with a quilt tucked around him. He rubbed his eyes, ran his fingers through his hair, flung the quilt aside and got up. It was after eight by the clock on the mantel.

The fire in the grate had died to ashes and embers, but the room was warm. He stepped to the dining room doorway and saw Mac lying exactly as he had last seen him, his eyes closed, his face peaceful. He was sleeping soundly and the blankets over his chest rose and fell with his regular breathing.

Ella came in from the kitchen. There were shadows beneath her eyes, but her figure was erect and her step lithe.

"Good morning, Andy. By the time you wash your face and comb your hair breakfast will be ready."

"You didn't rest at all," he said accusingly. He was ashamed of going to sleep and leaving her to face the long anxious night alone.

"I couldn't. I had a lot to think about. I sat beside you and watched the fire burn down, and time went fast."

"Was Mac all right?"

"He became restless once and muttered in his sleep, but most of the time he was quiet. You were the noisy one. You snored."

"Think how close you came to marrying me!"

She said, "That's one of the things I was thinking about."

He washed his hands and face and combed his hair in the bathroom upstairs, and when he came down he found bacon and eggs and toast waiting for him in the kitchen. He felt a deep sense of contentment as he watched her steady hand pour the coffee. They would have been sitting together thus every morning if he had not drifted so far from Red Rock these late years. Then, with a feeling that he was being disloyal to Mac, he wrenched his mind away from that subject.

"Sperry ought to be showing up."

"He said he'd come at eight. . . . Andy, where is Ralston Crane?"

He started. "Crane? How should I know? You might try his room at the hotel."

"I told you Mac was talking in his sleep. Most of it was a jumble, but a few words came out plainly. Once he shouted, 'Crane, you yellow-livered—'" She hesitated. "'Bastard,' he called him." Her eyes were pleading. "Did Crane shoot him?"

"I'm sure he didn't."

"Mac wouldn't tell me if it were so. He'd be afraid it would hurt me."

"Why should it? What do you care about Crane?"

She shook her head. "Nothing, Andy. Less than nothing."

Brant was a long way from understanding Crane's position in respect to the Macfarlane family, but he did not question her. He had no wish to pry; or, if the wish were there, no right.

"You can take my word that Crane didn't shoot him, didn't even see him last night. I talked with Mac and he trusts me, and if Crane had been around he would have mentioned it."

"He told you it was an accident?"

Brant fell back upon a subterfuge that, without being literally a falsehood, served the purpose of one. "I can quote him directly. His last words to me before you and Sperry saw him were, 'I was fooling with the gun and it went off.'"

That seemed to satisfy her.

Before they had finished breakfast Doctor Sperry arrived with his wife Agnes, who was thin and bespectacled and, except that stray wisps of blonde hair straggled from beneath her hat, resembled her husband almost comically. Agnes was going to help care for Mac and see to it that Ella rested.

"Damn' crazy woman'd work herself to death if someone didn't keep an eye on her," growled Sperry, referring to Ella. "Pair of fools is all they are—a grown man playing with loaded guns and his wife chasing around in blizzards in the middle of the night, both trying to get themselves killed."

Ella smiled wanly.

Brant borrowed Macfarlane's snowshoes for the walk to the *Reporter* office. Standing atop the drift that overflowed the front porch of the house, he slid his toes into the thongs, fitted the straps about the heels of his overshoes and stepped into a strange world.

The worst of the storm had passed, although the air was filled with feathery flakes. The wind was still strong enough to build drifts, but it was no longer a torture to face it. Unless the weather changed for the worse again, Red Rock could begin freeing itself from its fleecy straight jacket today.

It was going to be a man-sized job. The streets were flooded above the level of the highest porches and against some houses the snow was banked over the second-story windows. The branches of pine trees drooped and the trunks of some of the smaller ones were bent to the ground beneath their white burden, and would never stand straight again. A little way down the street children on skis were coasting down a granular mountain that leaned precariously against the side of a ramshackle barn.

In Superior Street a few people were out on skis and snowshoes, and several of them called and waved to Brant. Here and there men were digging down through the snow to reach the doorways of their stores.

A path had already been cleared to the doorway of the one-story *Reporter* building. Brant tramped down the crumbling incline, unbuckled the webbed frames from his feet and went in. Quarfield was sitting in a chair with his head in his hands and Carol was at her desk, tapping a portable typewriter.

"Greetings," Brant said. "Glenn, wherever did you get the ambition to shovel ten tons of snow this early in the morning?"

Quarfield lifted his head. His eyes were bloodshot and his face haggard and there was a looseness about his grin. "I woke up on your desk with a hangover and it was the only way I could get a drink. I spent the first third of the night in Oliphant's, the second third in Eckstrom's, and the third third here."

"Why didn't you go home?"

"I did once. I got my snowshoes and came back. Lola and me had some beer and I carried her home a little before midnight. I was close to my boarding house then, but I was so tuckered out I needed another drink. And after I'd got a couple more—"

"Skip the awful details," said Brant. "I get the general idea. Carol, did you manage to keep warm in that room?"

She looked up briefly from her work, her eyes aloof. "I did all right, thanks."

Something in her tone arrested him in the act of taking off his coat. "Anything the matter, Scoop?"

"She's in love," Quarfield grunted.

"May that day never come!" Carol said fervently. "No, Andy, nothing's the matter. How about you? Did you have a good night?"

"Terrible. I wound up sleeping in a chair at the Macfarlanes'. Mac shot himself."

She let her hands drop limply across the keyboard of the typewriter. Her expression of studied calm vanished as completely and swiftly as a design in chalk is erased from a blackboard by the use of a wet sponge.

"Mac what?"

"He was fooling with a revolver and got a bullet in the shoulder. Came within an inch of killing himself, but Sperry says he'll be all right. Ella found him in his office and he sent her for me."

"Oh, Andy!" Color flowed into her cheeks. "I—I didn't know."

"Of course you didn't. How could you? No one knows yet, unless Sperry did some talking this morning."

"I don't suppose," Quarfield said, "there's any chance it wasn't an accident?"

"What do you mean? That he might have shot himself purposely?"

"Folks have done it before. And then again, folks have been shot by other people. If I remember right, there was things said right in this room yesterday about a guy named Crane who might be heading for trouble with Mac."

Brant hung his coat and cap on the rack and stopped to unfasten his overshoes. He said, trying to sound casual, "I hope you don't go spreading anything like that. I know what happened, and I can tell you on the level that Crane didn't shoot Mac and Mac didn't try to commit suicide."

"Hell," Quarfield grumbled, "you'd think I was an old woman. I don't gossip."

"It's okay. I was just putting you right."

Carol's eyes were frightened. She said, "Andy, I have the most awful feeling that something is dreadfully wrong. I keep remembering what you said last night about picking this particular time to do any killing you might have in mind. I don't mean that you'd want to, but—"

His patience was near the breaking point. "Please, Carol, let's drop it. I think I also said there wasn't any sense in talking about murder unless we really had one. I have a lot of other things on my mind and one of them is the problem of getting out a paper without a linotype or power to run the press." He turned to Quarfield. "Come on, Glenn. Let's go out to the shop and see just how much space we're going to have to fill."

But he was not yet through talking about the Macfarlanes and Crane. Two or three minutes after he had left the front office the outer door slammed. A minute later Sheriff Ed Worth came into the shop, his blue eyes more watchful than usual, his lined face sterner.

"Quite a lot of snow we been having, Andy."

Brant's heart sank, but he strove to appear cheerful. "I thought I noticed some on my way to work."

"It was a bad night all around, they tell me—wind blowing and all that. I hear it was real chilly a little after midnight."

"It was, Ed. I was out in it."

"Yes, I know." The sheriff shook his head dolefully. "A bad night—with people getting shot and everything. I just stopped by to see Mac, but he was asleep. Now, Andy, what about Ralston Crane?"

So it was going to have to be discussed, after all. Brant sighed. "I don't know anything about him, except that a man named Rigby is up from Detroit to see him."

"I know that much. Rigby's staying across the street and isn't telling his business. Crane didn't get back to the hotel all night."

"He's not the only one. The saloons kept open house."

"Crane didn't show up at any of the saloons or at Gene Glebb's poolroom. Nobody I've talked to has any idea where he is. I called at Maggie Tucker's on a hunch, but the old girl was alone."

"I can't help you, Ed."

Worth took off his fur hat and massaged his gray hair with a mitten. "Mac told Ella and Sperry he shot himself by accident."

"I know. He was checking his gun and—"

"And it went off twice, which is a downright funny thing for a revolver to do accidentally. One bullet cut across the desk and hit the wall. Doc admits there was something queer about the one that got Mac. If he was holding the gun there ought to be powder burns on his clothes or his skin, but there wasn't any. The bullet went in at a downward angle, which means he must of been holding the gun high up in front of him."

"I wouldn't know about that."

"Another thing: fingerprints are out of my line—I leave that sort of business to the state troopers—but I got Ella to dig up the gun, which should never of been taken from the scene of the shooting in the first place, and looked over the smooth parts pretty close. I couldn't swear to it, but it looked to me as if it'd been rubbed with a damp cloth or else a man's bare hands."

Brant scuffed his feet. "When you handle a gun don't you run your hands over the barrel and metal parts? I've seen a good many men do it."

"Maybe a shotgun or a rifle, but you don't pet a thirty-eight revolver."

"What else is bothering you?"

"Well, there was a double trail of blood in the reception room. Why would he go to the door after he was shot, and then go back?"

"That's easy. He wanted to get home, or perhaps get help from the mill. Before he got outside he decided he couldn't make it. He went back to his office because there was a sofa he could lie down on."

"Uh-huh." Worth looked at the floor and at the ceiling. "I don't suppose you'll do it, Andy, but I wish you'd tell me why you're so set on covering up things about this shooting."

"What do you mean, covering up?"

"When I was in Mac's office this morning his chair was pushed against that hole in the wall and the phone book was over the bullet mark on the desk. The rug was scuffed and I guess it had been rumpled, but somebody had smoothed it out. Ella didn't do those things. She told me a chair was tipped over when she got there the first time. Doc didn't do any cleaning up. As far as I know you were the only other person alone with Mac."

There was a glint of admiration in Brant's eyes as he looked at Worth. The sheriff had never been trained in police methods, probably had never so much as read a book on the subject, and yet in his native shrewdness he missed nothing of importance.

"I did straighten the rug," Brant confessed, "and I did rearrange things a bit. I had a hunch Ella would be along with Doc Sperry. If she hadn't noticed the mess before—and I figured she might have been too excited to pay attention to anything but Mac—I thought it would be just as well if she didn't notice at all. But if I had really wanted to cover up I'd have got some putty and paint and done a job on those bullet marks, and changed one of those empty cartridges in the revolver for a good one after cleaning the chamber."

"How do you account for the rug being mussed?"

"Mac is a big man, Ed. He was badly hurt. He staggered and fell."

The sheriff's face crinkled in a friendly way. "You know, Andy, you grew up to be a right smart boy. Mac's a lucky man to have you for a friend. I'm his friend, too, but when something happens that doesn't look just right I'm duty bound to look into it, even if it does concern the most prominent citizen we got." He was abruptly stern again. "If there's been a criminal shooting, I want to find out about it. Sperry says Mac is apt to die. That talk of yours about murder and that talk of Carol's about Crane has got me thinking. I don't mind saying, in view of what's happened, that I don't like it a bit."

He turned toward the door, leaving Brant frowning after him, not liking it either.

7

Composing stick in hand, Brant bent over a type case, setting the first paragraph of the storm story in 14-point Cheltenham boldface. He knew the compartments of the tray and the mechanics of his task, for he had served his apprenticeship as a printer, but his fingers were clumsy from want of practice. He was glancing resentfully at the lifeless linotype machine when Carol came in from the office and handed him a sheet of paper. Through the open door the rasping voice of the battery radio was audible, talking through a crackle of static, monotonously reciting details of storm damage.

He read the typed lines. A snowplow out of Marquette had found a car buried in snow on the highway, and within it the frozen bodies of a man, woman and infant child.

"What else is coming?" he asked.

"The usual reports from outside about roads and tracks and wires. Here in town the roof of that old house of the Ryans' caved in and there was a small fire at Paul Cooney's. People keep bringing in items about the Parkers' cat freezing in the hencoop and the wind blowing a tree across Pedersen's woodshed."

"Forget the trivial stuff and hold everything else to short paragraphs." He raised his voice as she turned to go. "And Scoop. . . ."

"Yes?"

"Forget my barking at you a few minutes ago. I was worried about Mac."

"You didn't bark. You simply reminded me of what I've been told before. I talk too much."

"No, you don't. You're all right just the way you are."

Her eyes were disconcertingly direct. "Do you honestly think so?"

"I honestly do."

"Thanks, Andy." She gave him a smile before going back to her typewriter.

He returned to the slow business of selecting tiny blocks of metal and standing them on end in insecure rows, held in place by his left thumb. Quarfield, seated at another type case beside him, put down his stick to roll a cigarette.

Apropos of nothing, Quarfield said, "That bird from the city, Rigby, was in all the bars last night asking for Crane."

"Did he mention his business?"

"He wouldn't talk except to cuss the snow and let everybody know he thought they were nuts to live in a place like Red Rock—which is something him and I agree on. You know what I think? I think he's the law, sure enough, and Crane knew he was coming and beat it."

"Where could Crane beat it to?"

"If he was smart and had planned it ahead of time he could manage. There's half a dozen empty shacks and cabins in the woods close to town. A man could store grub and firewood there and lay low through the blizzard. When it was over he could start out with snowshoes and a compass, head for any station on the railroad and wait for the trains to run again."

"A timber cruiser could do it," said Brant. "A man who knows this country could manage. But Crane was raised in the city. What would he know about the woods?"

"A guy who didn't know what he was up against would be just as likely to try it as a guy who did," observed the printer, "only the scissorbill would probably wind up dead. I wouldn't give any odds, but I'd bet even money that if Crane didn't get home last night he's dead this minute."

Brant arose to fit the lines of type between column rules in the first-page form. "No use fretting about it till we know one way or the other."

"I wouldn't give a whoop in hell, only if he's dead I won't ever get that eighty bucks he lost to me last Saturday night. But then, I was never very sure of getting it anyway unless I took it out of his hide."

Quarfield could kiss his eighty dollars good-bye, Brant said to himself. Nobody but he and Mac would ever know for sure whether Crane was dead or alive, but his creditors would never see him again.

He felt in his pocket for his pipe and remembered that he had left it in his room. He had not thought of tobacco all morning, but suddenly he was aware of a longing for its soothing qualities. He told Quarfield, "Be back in a minute," and went into the office where his coat and hat hung.

Carol was at her typewriter, her white fingers flashing over the keys. She said, "A whole block of downtown Marquette is on fire and the hydrants are frozen. They're dynamiting buildings to try to stop it. That's worth some space, isn't it?"

"If the linotype was working it could have a column, but two paragraphs is the limit now. We'll give it the biggest display we can." Ordinarily it would have exasperated him to have to put his paper out in this slovenly fashion, but today the *Reporter* seemed less important than other things.

Already there was a vague trail from the door of the *Reporter* building to the other side of the street, broken by Ed Worth and other hardy adventurers who had visited the newspaper plant to get or give information. Brant followed it to the Northland Hotel. The lobby was deserted except for Nordquist, sound asleep in a wicker chair with his chin drooping on his chest and his web-fingered hands clasped over his stomach.

Brant climbed the stairs to his room, which was filled with a still cold that pierced deeper than that of outdoors. His pipe and oiled silk tobacco pouch lay on the dresser. He filled the briar bowl and struck a match, gazing contemplatively at his reflection in the mirror, marking the sharp lines of worry around his eyes and mouth. A couple more days of this, he mused, and he'd be as jittery as a hophead in jail.

It was then that he heard the faint sound through the wall that separated his room from Ralston Crane's—a stealthy shuffle followed by the complaining creak of a floor board. He waited, hardly breathing, listening with every nerve. After two or three seconds the sound was repeated, and then there was a sliding noise that could only have been made by a drawer being opened cautiously.

Brant went to the hall as quietly as he could and stood outside Crane's door. Through the pine panels the rustling of papers came distinctly, assuring him that he had made no mistake. Someone—Crane or another person—was in that room, and by the evidence of Brant's ears was searching for something.

He clamped his hand around the doorknob, holding it tightly to prevent its rattling, and turned it. The door was unlocked; it moved inward without resistance. Bracing himself against the unknown, Brant flung it wide and thrust his body into the opening, gripping his forgotten pipe in his left hand.

A man standing at the dresser with his back to the door whirled, choking back an exclamation. There was a clatter and a haze of white dust as his movement tipped over a tin of talcum powder, spilling the stuff across the top of the dresser. One of the dresser drawers was open; the man's elbow hit against its corner as his right hand jerked in the direction of his hip pocket.

"Ow!" cried Peter Rigby. Recognizing Brant, he checked the sweep of his hand. "What's the idea breaking in like that? What business have you got here?"

Brant stood against the edge of the door frame, his hands in his pockets, his jaw tight. He said, "That's one of the questions the sheriff will want to ask you. We have a law in these parts for the benefit of people who break into other people's rooms and tamper with their belongings."

"You don't need to tell me about the law." Rigby's smile tried to be at once ingratiating and defiant. "I'm law myself, see?" He pulled back the lapel of his coat to show a yellow metal badge pinned behind it.

Entering the room, Brant inspected the shield with interest. It was of bronze and was stamped with the words, "SPECIAL DEPUTY SHERIFF, WAYNE COUNTY, MICHIGAN."

"When I was a reporter in Detroit I had half a dozen of those," he snorted. "Every reporter in town had them, and every cheap politician, and everybody else who wanted one. You paid fifty cents and promised to vote for the sheriff at election time—but God help you if you ever tried to arrest anybody or pass yourself off as a regular staff deputy!"

"I was sworn in as an officer of the law—" began Rigby, blustering.

"Even if you were the sheriff's right-hand man in Wayne County," Brant broke in, "you're three hundred miles out of bounds at the moment. This is Red Rock County and the sheriff here is Ed Worth. He won't be amused to find you taking liberties in his territory without asking his permission. I wouldn't be surprised if he locked you up on a charge of breaking and entering, and if Judge Thorpe gave you about ninety days."

Rigby's eyes flickered. "Listen, Brant, there's no sense making a fuss about this. I'm not here to steal anything. All I want is information."

"What kind of information?"

"Well . . ." Rigby wet his lips. "It looks funny, don't it, Crane dropping out of sight just when I come up to see him? Folks tell me he wouldn't stay away from the hotel on a night like last night if he could help it. What if something happened to him, if there was foul play somewhere? I got a right—every citizen's got a right—to think about that and try to find out. Naturally I'd go to Sheriff Worth if I ran across anything."

"You're still guilty of breaking and entering, as far as I can see. I'm a pretty good citizen myself. It's my duty to turn you over to the authorities."

"For God's sake, don't do that! I came up here on legitimate business—legal business—and if I get in trouble it'll ruin everything."

Brant had no intention of causing Rigby's arrest. To do so, he reasoned, would instantly heighten interest in the disappearance of Crane and create a wave of curiosity and perhaps an official investigation that would seriously embarrass Mac and increase Ella's fears. It might be that Rigby's purpose in coming to Red Rock was closely related to the circumstances that had caused the trouble between Crane and Mac at the mill, and if that were so it would not help to make it public.

He suggested, "Maybe we can strike a bargain. You say you're after information. So am I. Tell me why you want to see Crane and I'll forget I found you in this room."

The other fidgeted. "I—it's a personal matter."

"I don't intend to print it."

"Just the same it isn't anything I can tell at this stage of the game."

"Is Crane in a jam, criminal or financial?"

"From what I hear he's been in a lot of them."

"That isn't what I asked."

Rigby said with a kind of hopeless desperation, "I'm not saying. I would, but I can't, and that's on the up and up. If you're not satisfied, call your sheriff—only I'm warning you it'll make trouble for a lot of people besides me. I wouldn't go to jail for being here, either, when the truth came out."

Brant recalled the involuntary movement of Rigby's hand toward his hip. "What if you went to jail for carrying a concealed weapon? That could get you a couple of years in the big house."

"I got a permit."

In the open drawer beside Rigby lay a sheaf of letters and papers bound by a wide rubber band. That, undoubtedly, was what Rigby had been after and would have had in another ten seconds, had not Brant interfered. It occurred to Brant that the bundle might explain the mystery of Crane's presence in Red Rock and his hold, if any, over John and Ella Macfarlane.

He would have given much to examine it.

"Outside, Rigby," he said, jerking his head toward the corridor. "I'm not a cop and I'm not going to turn you in, but I don't like to have extra-legal activities going on next door to me. If you want to search this room tell your troubles to Ed Worth. If he sympathizes he'll get the judge to sign a search warrant."

Sulkily Rigby obeyed, pausing in the doorway to make sure that Brant closed the drawer without removing any of its contents. Then when they were both in the hall and Brant had shut the door of Crane's room, the pudgy one went downstairs without a word. He did not pause in the lobby, but went through to the cafe.

Before going back to his office, Brant shook Eric Nordquist awake. He told the grumbling old man, "I want you to seal up Crane's room. I heard somebody prowling there a few minutes ago, but I think I scared him before he got anything."

Nordquist blinked stupidly. "Who was prowling?"

Brant skipped the question. "If I get a padlock, hasp and staple will you lock the door so it will stay locked?"

"I got them things, Andy. I'll put 'em on right away. Do you think it was this feller Rigby in the room?"

"It might have been. Take care of the padlock keys, will you, so nobody can steal them?"

"Nobody'll steal 'em from me. You reckon Crane's got valuables there?"

"Whatever he has must be valuable to someone. Don't waste any time."

"Right away. What do you think happened to Crane?"

Striding toward the door, Brant said, "How the devil should I know?"

"I bet he's dead," Nordquist called after him. "I bet somebody he treated dirty caught up with him in the storm. I bet—"

Brant slammed the door.

8

Half an hour after Brant had returned to his inexpert typesetting, men and machines began the arduous task of clearing the streets of Red Rock. Out from the county garage roared the big rotary snowplow, trade-named Snogo, to form the mechanized spearhead of a column of lesser plows and a small army of men with shovels who would collect two dollars a day from the town for their labor.

The rotary crawled on caterpillar treads, thrusting ahead of itself vertical knives that cut an eight-foot slice out of the solid white. Behind the knives whirled steel scoops that chewed the packed stuff into manageable chunks and hurled them upward and outward, so that a fat stream of snow arched constantly at the right of the contraption, piling over sidewalks and building fronts.

Starting at the west end of Superior Street, the Snogo clanked and clattered, advancing with ponderous difficulty, finding every inch of the way a battle. Deep drifts baffled it temporarily, holding it motionless while the steel treads slithered helplessly over the frozen pavement; at such times it would back away a few yards, its plume of snow thinning, and charge with thunderous fury again and again until it had battered its way to easier going.

Behind the rotary lay a lengthening corridor with straight glittering walls that might have been hewn from alabaster. At points where the discharge had blocked the entrance to homes and shops, the men who followed went to work with their shovels, digging through to doorways. Wherever possible they dug trenches, but there were places where the snow towered too high for that, and then they tunneled through.

Later, when it had cleared all the principal streets and done its share of opening the highway, the Snogo would return to widen the swathe of its first passage. Still later, when the inevitable thaw commenced, smaller plows would nudge the snow into mounds and trucks would cart away as much of it as possible. In two weeks, with luck and fair weather, the streets and highways would be in shape to accommodate their normal traffic.

The racket of the labored procession penetrated to the printing shop and brought Brant and Quarfield to the front door. Carol was already outside, watching with shining eyes, and Brant put his band on her shoulder.

"You can go home tonight, Scoop."

She pouted, "Supposing I don't want to? I never did get that heater you promised me."

"What good would it have done? There wasn't any current."

"It would have kept me from being lonesome. It would have reminded me of you."

He looked at her keenly. She was talking nonsense, and if there was any humor in her words it succeeded in escaping him.

"Sometimes I think you're a fairly bright girl," he muttered, "and then again I catch myself wondering how sane you are, if at all."

She laughed. "I'm crazy, Andy. Everyone else has known it for years and it's high time you found it out."

"All women are nuts," Quarfield stated glumly. "As a man of wide and varied experience I know."

"What about Lola?" Carol asked.

"She's nuts, too. Worse than that, she's driving me nuts."

"If you weren't batty to start with," Andy put in, "you wouldn't give a woman a chance to bother you. Take me—I swore off them when I was a kid. They don't worry about me and I don't worry about them, and everybody's happy."

"Oh, yeah?" Quarfield's grin was suggestive. "How about—?"

The rotary plow gave a sudden lunge forward just then and its motors made a deafening clatter, drowning out the printer's words. Brant wondered vaguely what the other had been going to say, doubting whether he would have had the nerve to mention Ella Macfarlane.

A twinge of something like pain went through him when he thought of her, and then the spectacle of the mammoth machine charging toward them across a space where the snow was uncommonly shallow claimed all his attention.

"Inside!" Quarfield shouted as the streams of snow came near. "You want to get buried alive?"

Brant waited for them to re-enter the office, followed, and closed the door as the frame building began to shake under the muffled thud of snow striking the roof. Almost immediately there was a rushing avalanche against the plate-glass windows. He half expected them to break under the pressure; but the force of the soft chunks as they fell was downward, rather than inward, and even when the windows were completely covered they showed no sign of strain.

Again Brant took down the oil lamp and lighted it. He said, "You had all that snow-shoveling for nothing, Glenn."

"No I didn't." Quarfield shook his head emphatically. "I had three snorts of liquor, and how I needed 'em! It was worth it. Just the same, it's your turn now."

Stuffing his pipe and firing it, Brant nodded. "I'll make a way out soon as they've gone past." Tilting back in his desk chair he waited until Quarfield had gone into the shop. He asked then, "Carol, did any of the people who dropped in this morning offer opinions about Mac getting shot?"

Her face was grave in the yellow lamplight. "All of them did. The story must have spread like an epidemic."

"What was the consensus?"

"That Ralston Crane shot him. Why Red Rock needs a newspaper, I don't know. Half an hour after you got here everybody had heard that Crane was missing and Mac was wounded and possibly dying. They'd heard, too, that there was bad blood between them. You know, it sounds like some of Agnes Sperry's broadcasting. And there's Rigby, who apparently hasn't made any secret of the fact that he's looking for Crane, and the general idea is that he's a cop."

"Did many of them say that? I mean about Crane shooting Mac?"

"All of them did," she repeated.

He smoked for a space in silence. Such rumors were bound to produce results. They would lead presumably to a systematic search for Crane and, when and if Mac was stronger, a focusing of suspicion upon him. That stalwart old fighter would take it in his stride, sticking to his story of an accident despite the evidence against it, or profanely hustling questioners on their way without troubling to tell any story at all. Ella, however, was made of more fragile stuff. She would see it through and never falter in her loyalty to the man she had married, but every ugly innuendo would cut her like a knife.

"Crane didn't shoot him," he said, knocking the ashes from his pipe against the base of the stove. "I'm sure of that. I'm pretty sure, too, that if I don't cut a hole through that snow we'll be here till May."

When he opened the door the snow banked against it faced him with a blank wall. He wielded a broad iron coal shovel, chopping great blocks out of the barrier and carrying them back into the shop. There was nothing to do but pile the stuff near a drain in the concrete floor and let it stay there until it melted.

As he got farther into the bank, crouching in a tunnel four feet high, he began to pile the loose snow behind him, so that the passage was nearly filled as rapidly as it was opened.

He had worked about three-quarters of an hour when the blade of the shovel punched through to daylight. A moment later he stood in the center of the street, breathing deeply from his exertions. He liked the novelty of the scene that met his eyes. In place of the familiar store fronts were doorways in the snow, some of them reinforced by planks, several bearing signs naming the establishments to which they gave admittance—for the oldest inhabitants of Red Rock might easily have become confused in the unfamiliar setting.

Willing hands, fueled by alcohol, had made short work of digging a wide and lofty tunnel from Oliphant's bar. The proprietor himself stood before it—a huge, black-haired man with a dirty white apron showing beneath his overcoat—affixing a square of cardboard to a stake driven in the snow beside the entrance. Crudely lettered upon the cardboard was the legend, "OLLIE'S IGLOO."

Oliphant glanced in Brant's direction. "How is business, Andy? Goin' to be able to put out a paper?"

"Going to put out something, Sam. Business is lousy, though. Nobody's doing anything right now except you and Eckstrom, as far as I can see."

The saloon owner shrugged. "'Tis an ill wind, they keep tellin' me. . . ." He disappeared into the tunnel, but his voice came back. "Stop by when ye get the chance an' have somethin' with me."

Brant shoveled his way back through his tunnel to the office, raising the ceiling to the height of his head, carrying the loose snow into the street and flinging it on the side of the sloping mound that all but swallowed the *Reporter* building. That took him another three-quarters of an hour.

In the meantime the rotary plow had found the going hard in the vicinity of the mill. For an entire block it had to contend with drifts higher than itself, and its progress was a series of short retreats and lumbering charges, each of which advanced it three or four feet. At the rate it was going, Brant estimated, it would not be able to open many streets before nightfall.

The narrow aisle in the center of Superior Street was populous. Men, women and children stood around in groups, entered and departed from stores, and here and there helped some merchant clear his passage through the snow. The scrape of shovels and the ring of voices merged with the incessant chatter of the Snogo. There was an air of enforced cheerfulness abroad, and Brant understood why people found the street preferable to the gloom of shrouded houses in the back streets.

He looked up and down for some sign of Charlie King, but did not see him, and did not think he would be in any of the saloons. Having shot Mac, King would be nursing his hangover out of sight today, he supposed, waiting to hear the worst. Unless he had been drunk enough and foolhardy enough to try to escape from Red Rock in his first panic following the shooting, he would be either in his room in the workingmen's boarding house that was glorified by the name Hotel Alger, or at some such hospitable establishment as Maggie Tucker's.

Quarfield had most of the material that would go into the newspaper already in type when Brant joined him. Brant busied himself with headlines, making them up as he stood at cases of 36- and 48-point type, sliding the metal blocks into a composing stick and changing his ideas on the spur of the moment when they did not fit.

He had barely begun this task when the biggest story of all broke without warning.

First came the sudden silence. Brant had not realized how completely the distant clatter of the rotary plow dominated other sounds until it ceased. For a second he heard plainly the ticking of Carol's typewriter, then that too stopped and it seemed that the world was utterly still.

Quarfield moved, the legs of his chair scraping on the concrete floor. "She went bust," he said.

But Brant was listening by that time to the shouting outside—the faint hail from the direction of the mill, the querulous answering cries, and finally the excited bawling up and down the street. It went on for seconds before his ears distinguished two chilling words:

"Dead man!"

He said, "They've uncovered something!" and sprinted for the door, snatching his cap and coat from their hooks in passing.

Carol was already in the street, buttoning her coat, looking toward the steel juggernaut that had halted in front of the mill. A few men had already gathered around the machine and others were hastening toward it, pouring out of the passages from stores and saloons. Ed Worth was on his way there, his short legs carrying him at a pace just less than a run; he cupped his mittened hands about his mouth and bellowed, "Don't none of you fellers touch nothing!"

Brant started walking swiftly toward the center of interest, feeling a dread so intense that he was hardly conscious of Carol clinging to his arm, panting in her effort to keep up with him. He shouldered his way through the knot of men at the front of the plow and stood by Worth, gazing at the curious object projecting from the unbroken snow ahead of the rotary scoops. It took him half a minute to realize that it was the stump of a man's leg, broken off below the knee, with a tatter of cloth fluttering around it and a jagged piece of bone jutting from the hard red flesh.

He swallowed and set his teeth, and when Carol whimpered he thrust her behind him.

There was sickness in the unshaven face and in the hoarse voice of young Merton Case, who had operated the plow. He said, "I was backin' out for a fresh start when I see a black thing kicked out with the snow. I didn't know what it was till it hit that tree and stuck there."

Case kept watching the ground, but all the others lifted their faces toward the ancient elm that spread its snow-covered branches at the corner of Mill Avenue. In the main crotch of the tree, plainly visible, was a black rubber-soled boot with three or four inches of a man's naked leg protruding from its top.

The sheriff said to Brant, "Give me a hand will you, Andy? We got to get him out of there."

Together they began to dig into the snow with mittened hands. Finally, when the body was uncovered to the waist they pulled together and the corpse slid out of its sheath—a nondescript figure crusted with white, its arms thrust downward and outward—and dropped into the soft snow at their feet.

It was Charlie King.

Brant glanced around the semi-circle of awed onlookers. Carol was hiding her face against the shoulder of some woman he did not recognize. Quarfield, who had stuffed his mittens beneath his arm, seemed less concerned than anyone else there. He was twisting a cigarette into shape.

"It was a bad night for drunks to go stumbling around," the printer volunteered. "Charlie found it out too late."

Something more violent than a combination of storm and liquor had overcome the mill worker, however. There were raw streaks in his face where claws or fingernails had ripped the skin. His eyes were open and bulging, his swollen tongue was visible between gaping lips and his cheeks were a mottled blue.

Worth opened the dead man's jacket and Brant saw the way the woolen scarf had been knotted around the throat. The knot was beneath the left ear, where King would never have placed it; and anyway King could not have fastened his own scarf that tightly even if he had wished to strangle himself.

The sheriff mumbled one word: "Murder." He straightened and for an instant his blue eyes met Brant's. Then he turned and looked for a long time at the stone office building of the paper mill.

Brant's mind balked there. He could not make himself think of his best friend and Ella's husband as the slayer of two men.

9

At a few minutes after one o'clock the electric bulbs in the newspaper shop came alight as suddenly as they had blinked out the night before. Brant looked up from his work thankfully, feeling somewhat as he imagined primitive man must have felt saluting the rising sun after dreary hours of darkness.

"There's service for you," he said to Quarfield, thinking of the linemen who had faced the dangers of the storm to locate and repair the breaks in the power cables. "Talk about your heroes—"

"They took their time," Quarfield grumbled. "I been all morning sticking type I could of run off in half an hour on the machine. We could be rolling the press now if they'd put the juice through sooner."

"If I had your disposition I'd keep it secret." Brant began lifting blocks of type out of the first-page form. "Get some metal melting and let's see if we can't do a decent job after all. I'm going to write the King and Macfarlane stories and some of the other stuff."

"We'll be here all afternoon."

The first copy of the *Reporter* came off the flatbed press shortly after four. Brant ran a critical eye over the headlines and the opening paragraphs of the main stories. It was a good looking front page, he decided, considering the haste in which it had been composed and assembled. If it was the most sensational newspaper ever published in the county—well, the news was the most sensational within the memory of any inhabitant.

The page was topped by three 96-point streamer lines which read:

CHARLES KING FOUND MURDERED;
MACFARLANE SHOT IN ACCIDENT;
CRANE FEARED LOST IN STORM!

Three separate stories dealt with the known facts of those occurrences—or such of the facts as Brant had seen fit to publish—but in his mind all of them ran together, just as the headlines tended to run together. No one, unless it was Macfarlane, knew better than he that they were actually three parts of the same story. Worth would suspect and Ella might guess, and people were bound to speculate, but the important thing was that the kernel of the truth remain hidden for the present.

As soon as he could, he left the shop and headed for Doctor Sperry's office. The rotary had left a clear path the whole length of Superior Street and had opened most of the intersecting avenues. Just now its racket was audible from somewhere in the vicinity of the courthouse on Commerce Avenue.

He found Frank Sperry occupying the cubbyhole that served as his consultation room in the yellow frame house where he lived with his wife and son. A wood fire muttered in an airtight stove in the center of the room, making the atmosphere oppressive with dry heat, notwithstanding which the doctor was muffled in a heavy brown sweater with a collar that hedged his ears. He was hunched over his rolltop desk, turning the pages of a magazine, and he frowned at Brant through his horn-rimmed spectacles.

"I'm here for the day and maybe the week," he growled. "Half the town can die and the other half have babies and I wouldn't budge out of this chair. I tell you I'm too damned old for this chasing around in the middle of the worst night of the last thousand years."

Brant dropped into a chair, ignoring the outburst. He asked quietly, "How about him, Doc?"

"How about him! He's dead, that's all. Finished, deceased, defunct, departed. He was hit on the head with something and then he was strangled, as any fool could see. It's just as well, considering that he was drunk all the time."

"Oh," said Brant. "Oh, yes." He had partly risen from his chair, but he sat down again and relaxed. "You mean Charlie King. I was asking about Mac."

"Why don't you make yourself plain? That old lunatic will live if he wants to. I told you so last night. Except for his head he's sound as a Lake Superior cliff. But he's got to take orders from me, and if he blows off that temper of his once more I'm going to give him up and turn the case over to Coroner Perrault."

Besides being the county coroner, Simon Perrault was Red Rock's leading undertaker.

"How is Ella?"

Sperry smirked. "I tricked her. She wouldn't lie down, so I made Agnes fix her a cup of coffee and slipped enough barbital in it to knock out an elephant. When I left there an hour ago, after checking over King's cadaver and fighting with Mac about whether he should stay in bed or not, she was dead to the world. She shouldn't come out of it till seven or eight o'clock. Meanwhile Agnes is in charge and I've got to fix my own supper."

"Funny how he shot himself," Brant ventured.

"Listen." The physician leaned forward and tapped Brant's knee with a skinny forefinger. "One reason I had trouble with Mac was because he wouldn't tell me the truth. A patient can't get along with a doctor by lying to him. He didn't shoot himself. I told the sheriff so and I'm telling you, just like I told him. If you want to get kicked right out of my house just try to argue with me about that."

"Isn't there a chance—?"

"Not a ghost of a chance."

"Then why would he say so?"

"Andy, I'm not an officer of the law nor even a particularly conscientious citizen. I'm too busy to worry about moral problems. I gave Ed Worth my opinion of how the bullet wound was inflicted because Ed asked for it and in his position he's entitled to it, but I haven't told anyone else and I won't. As a special favor to you I'll go even further. You asked why he said it was an accident?"

"I did."

"All right. He said it because Charlie King was lying dead in the snow outside and Mac hoped he wouldn't be found there."

"Wait a minute, Doc. Are you trying to make a case against Mac for murdering King?"

"I'm not trying to make anything. You form your own opinion and I'll form mine, and Ed Worth can form his. It doesn't worry me much. In fact it worries me so little that I didn't bother to tell Ed that when I was washing Mac up last night I found some shreds of human skin under his fingernails. They might just possibly have come from those scratches in Charlie King's face."

Brant got up. "Good God, Doc, I don't know what to do!"

"Don't do anything. You can't change what has already happened. Just keep your mouth shut and hope for the best. Mac's a hard man to reason with, but I've been his friend most of his life and I'm not going to say anything that could make trouble for him. The only reason I've talked to you is because you're his friend too."

"Thanks." The young man turned toward the door. "I'm going to pay him a visit."

"Not yet. I gave him the same dose I gave Ella and they both should be asleep. Wait till after supper. And when you do go, see if you can find out something for me."

"What's that?"

Sperry's waspishness had departed. Now he was only a worried little man sitting in a creaky swivel chair with a brown sweater enveloping him. He removed his glasses and breathed gently on the lenses.

"I suppose I'm about the best doctor in the Upper Peninsula, but I can't do much for a patient who won't co-operate. Will you try to find out why Mac doesn't want to keep on living?"

Brant stiffened. "What makes you think he doesn't? Did he say so?"

"He didn't have to say so. He showed it in a dozen ways. There's something on his mind that hasn't anything to do with Charlie King. At least, when I told him what had happened to Charlie and went into the subject at some length, he didn't react the way I think he would have if that had been his big trouble."

"Haven't you any idea?"

"It might be connected with a stranger in town, a man who calls himself Rigby. He paid Mac a visit before I did."

"Rigby!"

"That's right. I understand he's been trying to find Ralston Crane. According to Mac that was his only reason for calling there, but at the rate Mac is lying you can take it or leave it."

"Rigby had a lot of nerve bothering a sick man."

"I left word there were to be no visitors except you. Ella and Agnes tried to keep him out. Unfortunately Mac was awake and heard the talk at the door. He insisted on seeing the guy."

"I'll try to find out what's on Mac's mind and talk him out of it," Brant promised. A cold desperation came over him. "We can't let him die, Doc!"

Sperry hooked the frames of the glasses behind his ears and began turning the pages of his magazine. "We'll do what we can, son."

Brant walked aimlessly along Superior Street, deaf to the greetings of people he passed. If Mac did not want to live, it seemed to him it could only be because he was unwilling to run the risk of being called to account for two homicides. In trying to escape through the door of death Mac would not be thinking of himself—he had no personal fear whatever—but would be hoping to protect the girl he loved from the shame and disgrace that would attend a murder investigation whether or not guilt could be proved. Yet while Ella might be hurt if Mac should be accused of murder, officially or by wanton tongues, that would be nothing compared with the crushing blow his death would deliver. Clenching his fists, Brant told himself that Mac must never be permitted to make the sacrifice.

The muffled banging of a door, the sound of scuffling and a chorus of profanity broke in upon his meditations. The noise issued from the snow tunnel that led to Sam Oliphant's bar. It rose in volume for a space, then subsided, and Oliphant's voice roared:

"Outside, ye slanderin' snake! Out ye go, an' if ever ye come back I'll cut ye in pieces an' feed ye to the dogs!" There was the solid *thwack* of a swung club coming in contact with a cushioned part of the human anatomy.

As Brant watched, more curious than alarmed, a hulking figure in an old tan overcoat came staggering out of the tunnel, took half a dozen steps into the street and halted. It was Big Al Nowka, whom the sheriff had classed among the trouble-makers of the community.

A laborer at the Wessendorf sawmill, Nowka was six and a half feet of Polish brawn and muscle. Normally he was as harmless and friendly as a puppy, with simple laughter in his blue eyes and on his thick lips; but a certain amount of whiskey invariably worked a transformation in his character. Drunk, he would fight on the slightest pretext—or none at all—with the strength and ferocity of a gorilla, and frequently three or four men would be seriously injured before he was subdued. He also had a disquieting habit of seizing women in the streets and endeavoring to disrobe them; an ambition in which he had never quite succeeded, so far as anyone knew, due to the invariable proximity of some male chivalrous enough to risk a mauling for a lady's virtue.

Nowka was drunk today. He wheeled to face the mouth of the tunnel; his shoulders bent forward and his long arms dangling. Blood streamed from a cut on his forehead, his eyes blazed and his lips were drawn tightly back from his teeth.

Sam Oliphant appeared in apron and shirtsleeves, brandishing the baseball bat with which he pulverized the ice that chilled his beer coils.

"On yer way!" the saloon keeper ordered. "Git along down the street or so help me I'll bash yer damn' brains out!"

For a second it looked as if Nowka would spring upon the other, but when Oliphant swung the club viciously the big man jumped back. He mouthed words of Polish, then lurched down the street toward Eckstrom's bar, his feet wide apart.

Oliphant noticed Brant. He said, "I been just waitin' fer the big ape to make trouble. He was drinkin' since last night, singin' an' carryin' on, an' gettin' mean every time I told him he'd drank enough. All of a sudden there was hell to pay. He cold-cocked three customers before I could lay the pacifier on him. So help me, he's goin' on the Indian list fer good."

"What started it?" Brant asked.

"They was some talk about the killin'. Big Al gets up an' says Macfarlane killed Charlie King an' Crane too. Nowka hasn't got no use for Mac since he was fired from the paper mill fer bein' drunk a year ago. He called Mac some hard names an' there was boys from the paper mill at the bar, an' they wouldn't stand for it."

"Who tackled him?"

"Jim Scott took the first wallop an' got slammed in a corner fer his pains. Tony Brinker busted two chairs throwin' 'em. I didn't rightly see who else was fightin' an' who was tryin' to hide in the privy."

Scott, Macfarlane's night engineer, came out to the street, rubbing his jaw. His eyes were smoldering.

"Next time I'll take a pipe wrench to the bastard," he vowed. "No man, drunk or sober, has got the right to say what he said about a man who may be on his deathbed this minute."

Brant took in the engineer's slim wiry figure. "You'll get yourself killed tackling them that size."

"I damn' near did. I think my jaw's broke. Just my luck if it is."

"It ain't broke," said Oliphant. "You was leanin' away from the punch."

"I do have the damnedest luck," Scott mumbled. "Nobody remembered to bring my overcoat back from Mac's after the shooting, and when I was ready to quit work this morning I found someone had took my cap and one of my mitts from my locker down in the pulp mill. I had to wrap up in burlap sacks to keep from freezing to death." He asked plaintively, "Now who would want to steal my cap and one mitt?" Brant could think of one person who might have needed those things, and the thought opened a new and tempting field of conjecture.

What if Ralston Crane had not died in that log chopper after all?

10

Quarfield was sitting with Lola Tucker in a booth in a back corner of the Northland Cafe when Brant and Carol arrived there for dinner. Quarfields's arm was about the dark girl's waist and something in their expressions suggested to Brant that all was not well.

Carol noticed it too. She said, sliding into another booth, "The course of true love doesn't seem so smooth today."

"Both of them drank too much last night," Brant suggested. "I've had the same thing the matter with me."

It was more involved than that, however. When Lola came to take their orders he saw that her cheeks were pallid under their rouge, her eyes sullen and her hands tremulous. A livid scratch crossed her forehead and two blue bruises showed against the ivory of her throat.

"What happened to you?" he asked bluntly. "You weren't in that fight next door, were you?"

Her black eyes were stony. "No, I wasn't. What are you going to eat?"

"Pardon me for being interested," he said, studying the menu. "Carol, what do you say to Virginia ham and candied yams?"

"Reminds me of the sunny south. Order them, Andy."

91

"On two, Lola." He watched the half-breed girl as she went toward the kitchen, her body swaying gracefully. Then his glance swerved to Quarfield, who sat with his chin propped on his fist, staring broodingly at nothing.

"I'll bet they had a fight," Carol whispered. "Do you think he might be brute enough to choke her?"

"I couldn't say." He would not put it past Quarfield, given the proper provocation—or past Lola to provoke him—but his speculations were taking account of other possibilities.

If Ralston Crane were alive—if he had slipped out of the mill while Macfarlane was unconscious, leaving his own cap and mitten and appropriating Jim Scott's—he would be hiding in Red Rock this minute; and what more convenient place to hide than Maggie Tucker's ramshackle establishment? The fact that the sheriff had made inquiries there and learned nothing was not to be considered conclusive. A woman whose property abounded in caches for illicit whiskey would have no difficulty in concealing a man.

In that case, Lola would of necessity have been admitted to the secret. She might have disapproved of Crane's presence, and been manhandled by him in his anxiety to impress upon her the importance of keeping silent. Or perhaps Crane had resorted to violence for a more primitive reason.

It made a pleasing theory, with Rigby's arrival providing in some still-to-be-explained way the motive for Crane's wish to disappear. As for Charlie King and his fateful attempt to blackmail Macfarlane—it was conceivable that King had not witnessed the fight between Crane and Mac at all, but had reached the head of the log conveyor in time to overhear Brant's suggestion that Crane had been killed. That, plus the evidence of the scarlet hunting cap and the fur-lined mitten, would have been enough to start

King's avaricious mind working on a plan for profit.

Going a step further into the realm of conjecture, what valid cause was there not to suppose that King had been murdered for his interference not by Macfarlane, but by Crane?

Carol's soft voice interrupted the wishful progress of his hypothesis. She said, "Andy, I have a confession to make. Last night, about midnight, I heard a knocking sound and got up. Someone was at your door."

"It was Ella."

"Yes. I know. It was dark, but I recognized her in that white outfit. I—I stayed there at my door watching."

"Well?"

"She was in your room for a long time. Then both of you came out and you had your arm around her."

He was embarrassed. "She told me what had happened to Mac and I had to put on some clothes before I could go with her. She was exhausted by what she had been through and I had to put my arm around her to keep her from falling." He went on, thinking of himself getting dressed, "It was even darker in my room than in the hallway."

"Oh, I understand all that. The thing is, I didn't understand it at the time. I didn't sleep. I lay awake imagining the most awful things."

"You mean you thought we—?" He regarded her incredulously. "My God, Scoop, what a mind you have! Ella is the wife of my best friend."

She sighed. "A lot of us women have dirty minds. Glenn was right when he said all of us were nuts. But I know how wrong I was and I'm ashamed. I want you to know I'm sorry and I hope you'll forgive me.

"There's nothing to be sorry about. There was no harm done." He was puzzled by her behavior. Why had she worried in the first place about whether there could be anything like that between him and Ella? Why had she decided,

when her mind was finally set at rest, that she must con-
fess and ask his pardon?

It would be more easily comprehensible if Carol were
in love with him and therefore jealous of Ella, but under
the circumstances. . . . He smiled inwardly at his ridiculous fancy.

"Coffee?" inquired Lola, placing silver and crockery on
the porcelain table with clattering carelessness. He nodded and she moved toward the nickel-plated urn behind
the counter.

"What's the program for tonight?" he asked Carol, feeling a need for light conversation. "Going home, or going
to celebrate the finish of another week?"

"If there are passes at the office I'm going to the Idle
Hour Theater. I meant to ask you earlier. A movie ought
to give my brain a rest."

"Not this movie. Do you know what's showing?"

She inclined her head. *"Down Among the Dead Men,* a
hair-raiser. Are there passes?"

"Sure, if you think you can stand it. You saw one dead
man today, though. Aren't you ever satisfied?"

She shivered. "That one was real. It's different in the
movies. You know it's a game and no matter how hopeless
things look, everything will come out all right. You're never
really scared, but you get a thrill just the same, and it's
good for you because it lets out emotions that might make
you wacky if you bottled them up." Her lips curved. "I
didn't figure that out for myself; I read it in an article by
a psychologist, so there may be something to it."

"You win," he said. "The passes are yours. If I didn't
have to pay a visit to the Macfarlanes I'd go with you." He
was impatient to see Ella and her husband and discover,
if he could, Mac's reason for not wanting to get well. If
it had to do with Crane, Brant's new theory rejecting the
notion of a shredded body in the pulp vat might change

the wounded man's point of view. If it was something else entirely, he and Ella together might be able to work out a cure.

At the office he found the passes sent around each week by the Idle Hour Theater. He gave them all to her. "Take somebody with you," he said.

"There isn't anyone I'd like to be with. It would be fun if you could go, though."

"If it wasn't for Mac I would." He looked at his watch and saw that it was nearly seven. "Now run along, Scoop. You can be in time for the first show and get to bed early. Have a good time."

He saw her slim figure silhouetted briefly against the pale glow of street lamps beyond the tunnel. She was an unpredictable youngster, but a completely likable one. One of these days she would make a fine wife for some lucky man, he supposed; although he could not think off-hand of any marriageable man in Red Rock who was good enough for her.

He had turned off the lights in the office and opened the door to leave when a figure swung in from the street. "Got a minute, Andy?" Quarfield asked.

Brant switched on the lights. "What's bothering you, Glenn?"

"Big Al Nowka." Quarfield threw a leg over a corner of Carol's desk and glowered. "There's a man who ought to be strung up by the ears."

"I thought they took the fight out of him when they kicked him out of Oliphant's a couple of hours ago. Has he been making more trouble?"

"I hate to run to the law, but I'm going to get Ed Worth to lock him up."

"Let's hear the worst."

"Did you happen to see those marks on Lola's face and throat?"

"I was wondering about them."

"Nowka left 'em there. He came into the restaurant a while ago, crazy drunk. Nobody was in the place besides Lola, except Merckel, the cook, in the kitchen. Nowka grabbed her by the throat and hit her when she tried to break loose. He ripped the uniform she was wearing clear off and had her bent back over a table when Merckel heard the racket and came running out with a knife. Nowka had sense enough left to be scared. He beat it. As soon as Lola got over being hysterical she put on another uniform and went back to work, but she's so upset she's liable to go to pieces any time."

"Worth will see that it doesn't happen again," Brant said. "Look for him at the courthouse. If I see him I'll tell him about it."

So Crane could not have put those marks on Lola, and there went one of the lesser props of his inspired theory. Of course, Brant reflected, it by no means followed that because Crane had not beaten Lola, he was not alive and in hiding; nevertheless he felt a sense of disappointment.

"By the way," he asked, "when you got to Lola's place last night, did you go inside?"

"For half a minute," Quarfield said. "To get warm."

"Who was there?"

"Not a soul except the old lady, and she was in bed snoring. That place is too far out of the way for anybody to go to in a blizzard."

"Are you sure?"

"Well, if anybody *was* there, Andy, it was somebody who was careful to keep out of sight."

11

The rotary had been through Alger Avenue and someone had cleaned the sidewalk and porch of the Macfarlane house. The falling snow had laid a half-inch carpet since then and in the light that came from the living room windows narrow footprints were visible, pointing away from the steps. They meant, Brant deduced, that Agnes Sperry had gone home to see to the needs of her own family, which in turn meant that Ella was awake.

She came to the door in answer to his ring. She cried, "Andy, I was worrying about you. I hoped you'd come earlier."

"I would have, but Sperry said you were sleeping and I didn't want to wake you." He went into the light where he could see her face plainly, and was shocked. There were blue circles under her eyes and fine lines in the forehead and beside the mouth. "Didn't you rest at all?"

"Not much. Doctor Sperry must have given me some medicine without my knowing it, because I slept for two or three hours and now I feel fuzzy. All the time I slept I dreamed that Mac was dying. Agnes said I tossed around and moaned every minute."

He pitied her with all his heart. "What can I do to help, Ella?"

"Make him well," she said. "Make him realize how important it is that he gets well. That's all I need."

"How is he now?"

"Sleeping—or he was two minutes ago."

"Sperry said something about a mental depression—about some screwy notion of Mac's that he isn't going to come out of it."

She sank down on the sofa, motioning to Brant to sit beside her. She spoke just above a whisper.

"He has a strange, idea, Andy. You must try to convince him it's a wrong one."

"What kind of an idea?"

She seemed oddly confused. "He'll tell you when he wakes up. Don't be embarrassed by anything he says. He thinks he's doing what is best for you and me. He—he wants to die for *us!*"

He stared at her. "He must be crazy. The shock must have affected his mind."

"No, his mind is clear. Too clear, perhaps, and too determined."

"A man named Rigby was here. Could he have had anything to do with the way Mac feels?"

"I don't believe so. Mac was talking about . . . this thing . . . before Rigby came. I understand Rigby is trying to get in touch with Crane." Her face twisted. "Andy, what happened to Ralston? I have to know!"

"You can guess as well as I. He hadn't ever run into a storm like this one. He didn't know how dangerous it was to be out in it. He might have frozen to death."

"No. I happen to know that Ralston went into the mill right after work stopped yesterday to see Mac about a . . . a personal matter. I begged him not to because I was afraid Mac would lose his temper and hit him. Ralston went into the mill and no one has seen him since!"

"Ella, you mustn't think—"

"How can I help thinking? Last night Mac was shot, and from the way Doctor Sperry and the sheriff acted I don't believe they're willing to accept it as accidental. Today Charlie King was found murdered a hundred feet from where the shooting took place. Don't you see?"

"I see you jumping to conclusions. I don't like to see you being suspicious of Mac, if that's what you are."

"Must men always be stupid? It isn't suspicion. I want to know the truth. Do you think it matters to me—to the real me that promised to love and honor Mac, and meant it—what he may have done? He's my husband and I want to help him. Do you think I'd turn against him if I learned he was a . . . a . . ."

"Say it. If it's in your mind, get it out."

"A murderer."

He leaned toward her. "Pay close attention to what I'm going to say, Ella. Mac is not a murderer. As sure as you and I are sitting here—"

The creaking of bedsprings in the next room stopped him. There was silence for half a minute, then Mac's voice boomed out, surprisingly strong for that of a sick man:

"Who's a murderer?"

Ella went quickly to the double doors that were between the rooms. "Andy's here to see you, Mac, We've been waiting for you to wake up."

"Wake up! I've been lying here counting flyspecks on the ceiling and listening to you for hours. Send that young punk in here!"

She gave Brant a warning glance and put a finger to her lips. He reassured her with a nod, entering the room.

He said, "You old rhinoceros, if I didn't think you were lying about being awake I'd tell Sperry to double the dope he's been giving you."

Mac grinned wryly. His hair was matted, his bearded face was gray and sunken, but there were live coals in his eyes.

"That dope has got my head spinning like a top. You'll find a bottle of Scotch in the pantry. Pour one for yourself and make mine a big one."

Brant perched on the edge of the bed. "Not on your life. You've got too much energy for a sick man as it is. Two drinks and you'd be yelling for your clothes."

"Why not?" Mac tried to heave his body up in the bed and a quiver of pain distorted his lips. Brant raised his head and propped pillows beneath it, and Mac went on, "A man never knows how many enemies he's got till he's flat on his back. Then, when he can't defend himself, all the ones he thought were his friends start making him miserable. They cut off his liquor when he needs it worst; they fill him up with pills that make him dizzy; they give him hell because he wants to enjoy what little time he's got left."

"That's what you get for playing with guns. Next time you'll be more careful."

"Next time . . ." Mac did not finish what he had started to say. Instead he slanted his eyes toward Ella. "Darling, will you leave us alone for a few minutes? You'd better shut the doors so I can talk freely without curling your ears."

Her smile may have been forced, but it had a shining quality that transformed her. "Gladly, Mac. I have a million things to do; they've been piling up while I've been keeping an eye on you. Slap him down if he makes a false move, Andy, and holler if you need help."

As the door closed behind her, Mac mumbled huskily, "God never made a finer person."

"We won't argue about that. You ought to be the happiest man in the world."

"I was."

Brain took a cigar from the box on the bedside table and put it in Mac's mouth. He got out his pipe and tobacco pouch.

"You will be again before many days. I had a talk with Sperry this afternoon. He says a machine gun couldn't stop you. He says you'll be too pig-headed to lie down when the world comes to an end."

"He does, eh?" Mac bit the end from the cigar and sucked on it, drawing in the flame of the match Brant held for him. "Sperry is an incurable liar like all doctors. They think they can tell their customers anything and get away with it, but a doctor doesn't know a thing about a patient that the patient doesn't know better, unless he's an imbecile. This is my finish, Andy. I feel it in here." He tapped his chest.

"I never thought you were a quitter," Brant chided. "I never expected to hear you talking like a baby because you stopped a slug. It didn't hit a vital spot or smash a bone."

"You forget the shock and loss of blood. I'm not a kid like you and Ella."

"When will you be a hundred?"

"Forty-six years and three months from now; but I've crowded plenty of living into fifty-four years. I've worked hard and fought hard and drank hard, and important parts of me are worn out."

"Your guts, maybe. You wouldn't be talking like this if you had any left. You'll be playing a dirty trick on your wife if you don't pull yourself through."

"That's where you're wrong."

Brant braced his elbow on a crooked knee. "Mac, if you're worrying about our friend Crane, I have good news for you. There's a first-class reason to believe that he didn't go into the chopper at all, but is only hiding from this man Rigby."

"Go on," the other said, his eyes narrowing.

"When I found you passed out after your fight, Crane's cap and one of his mittens were on the floor outside the foreman's office. Charlie King took them away, you remember."

"So you told me. I didn't see 'em."

"It's the truth. Well, they weren't the only ones that disappeared. When it was time for Jim Scott to go home next morning he opened his locker and found that some-one had swiped his cap and one of his mitts. Do you see what that means?"

"I'm not sure I do. You think Crane swiped them?"

"Who else?"

"Why didn't he take his own?"

"Because," Brant said, "he wanted it thought he had been made into pulp. He knew Rigby was after him and he didn't want to face the music."

"But King claimed he saw me throw him in—"

"All King saw was a chance to make some money. He knew, one way or another, that Crane was alive, but was playing dead. It looked like a chance for him to cash in and skip town on a bankroll provided by you."

Mac smoked in silence for a moment. "People are say-ing I killed King. They're not fooled by my story about an accident. They think he shot me, which is true, and that I strangled him, which isn't true. The best I could do was grab for him and scratch his face a little before he put a bullet in me."

"So you scratched his face." There, Brant thought exul-tantly, was the logical explanation of those shreds of skin beneath Mac's fingernails that had made Sperry think he had killed King. "And how do you know people are saying you killed King?"

"Rigby told me."

"He's a crook if I ever saw one. Mac, a drunken man in Oliphant's saloon said at five o'clock today that he thought you had killed King. At one minute after five he was out-side in the snow with a gash in his head and sore spots all over him. There was a bunch of your workmen in the place and they wouldn't stand for any talk like that. That's the kind of friends you have in this neck of the woods."

"They were drunk and spoiling for a fight. I just furnished them with an excuse."

"You shouldn't low-rate loyalty that way. What did Rigby come here for?"

"He said he thought I might know where he could locate Crane. His story is that Crane forged a flock of checks before he came up here and his job—Rigby's—is to pinch him."

"Rigby is only a special deputy sheriff in Detroit, which means he has considerable less authority than a dog-catcher. When the law goes after a fugitive the usual procedure is to wire the local authorities to hold him. Then a city or state cop or a staff deputy sheriff, depending on who wants the culprit, is sent to bring him back. Oh, yes—and there has to be a warrant."

"Rigby showed me a warrant for Crane."

Brant frowned. It was not impossible that Rigby was in town on legitimate business, he realized, although he found that theory difficult to accept.

"You told me everything last night, didn't you, Mac?"

"The whole works. My head was clear as a bell right up to the time Ella found me. I didn't kill King. We wrestled for a minute before he shot me. Later I chased him as far as the door, then crawled back. If I'd gone out in the snow I'd be there yet."

"So who did the murder if it wasn't Crane?"

The mill owner stirred restively. "It's good of you to try to cheer me up, but you haven't got a leg to stand on. Just because Scott lost a cap and mitten and Crane did too, you want to make something of it. It doesn't prove anything. For all we know King might have taken Scott's stuff just to ball us up."

"But looking at it reasonably—"

"What's the use? If I didn't kill Crane I'm sorry. I'd do it now if I had the opportunity. I'm all washed up and it would be a final good deed before I cashed in my chips. I wasn't kidding about the way I felt. I don't mind dying. I haven't missed much in life."

Sensing the imperviousness of the man's will, Brant despaired of making a dent in it. But he had to try.

"What will become of Ella without you?"

"I'm sort of counting on you to look after her, Andy."

"Me! I'd be a poor substitute for you, Mac. She wouldn't appreciate the switch.

"You know better than that. It was a mistake, my marrying her in the first place. I'd have made her a better father than husband, and if I hadn't been too lonesome to think straight I'd have known. But it isn't too late to rectify it."

Consternation went through him like high-frequency current. "For Christ's sake, Mac—!"

"I know how you feel toward each other. It shows good sense in both of you. I'm honestly happy about it. I think the world of the pair of you and it eases my mind to know you'll be looking after each other when I'm out of your way."

"Out of our way!" He choked on the words. "You crazy old fool, both of us would go through hell barefoot for you! Ella loves you, and if you weren't out of your head you'd see how you're hurting her by acting this way.

"Now listen to me, Mac. I have a couple of things to say and I wish you'd let me get them said without interruption. The first is, you're off the track farther than you've ever been in your life. Ella and I had a college romance that took a year or two to die out. There was one nice thing about it: we've stayed friends and probably always will. If ever I can do anything for her I'll do it, just as I'd do anything I could for you. But that's the end of it, and if it wasn't intended to be the end we'd never have drifted so far apart.

"The second thing is: You may be older than Ella, but you've given her what I could never give any woman—the ideal of a strong, unselfish, self-reliant man, one she can lean on and count on no matter what happens. Compared to you I'm a kid just finding out about life, with most of my mistakes ahead of me. She has anchored herself to you and as long as you stay put she knows she'll never have to be afraid of anything. And this thing I know: if you slide out on her now she'll miss you for the rest of her life, and nobody on God's green earth will ever make her stop missing you."

Mac dropped his cigar into the tray on the table by the bed. He said, "You should have been a preacher. I never knew you could be so sentimental and at the same time make it sound so convincing."

"Think it over, will you?"

"Why not? I've thought about it a lot, but I can think some more if Frank Sperry doesn't dope me up too much."

"Every word of what I said is the truth," Brant told him earnestly.

Mac put out his hand and Brant grasped it. The wounded man's clasp was strong, and in some way it seemed to reflect the stubbornness of the spirit behind it and make Brant sadly aware that he had not been convincing enough.

Later, when he had a moment alone with Ella, he told her what Mac had said. "If he should die—willfully, I mean, for my sake," she moaned, "I couldn't ever be happy."

"Tell him that, Ella," he said. "Tell him over and over. Make him believe it."

12

Doctor Sperry was late in arriving. He stamped into the Macfarlane living room at ten, puffing like a winded horse, and dropped his satchel unceremoniously on the floor as he fumbled with the buttons of his overcoat.

"Town's gone mad," he observed gruffly. "Lib Turner busted her leg on the cellar steps, the Bookman boy has got pneumonia and May Berger expects her seventh baby before morning." He stuck out his chin, glowering through misted spectacles at Ella. "You're sick too. Why the devil didn't you sleep?"

"I did."

"Not enough. I'll fix it for you tonight, though." He lowered his voice. "I'm going to give that cantankerous old husband of yours some quadruple-strength knockout pills. After I get through with him he won't move an eyelid for ten hours."

"Won't they hurt him?"

"What a question! I'm a doctor, a good one, the best in a hundred miles or more, and my prescriptions never hurt anybody. They'll do him good and keep him out of mischief. Do you good too, by giving you a chance to quit worrying about him." He said, "If there was a nurse in town or anybody with sense enough to look after things

I'd get her, but there's only Agnes and she's got to sleep once in a while."

"Promise to go to bed, Ella?" Brant pleaded. He hated to think of her sitting up alone in the house through the long night. He would have stayed, except that he felt it might not be wise in view of Mac's state of mind.

"I promise," she said.

Sperry sidled nearer to Brant. "What did you find out?" he whispered.

Over the physician's shoulder Brant watched Ella. A warning look came into her eyes and she gave her head a barely perceptible shake.

"I don't know, Doc." He hunched his shoulders and dug his hands into his pockets. "Mightn't he be just tired and discouraged? Don't you think he'll snap out of it in a day or two?"

Sperry snorted in disgust. "Fine cooperation I get! Bullets don't faze me, or fractures or germs or babies, but a conspiracy of silence makes me want to poison everybody in sight, including myself. If you're through shushing Andy, Ella, you can heat some water. I'm going to have a look at that dressing. He doesn't have to get well if he doesn't want to, but at least I can make sure that he isn't helped along in his foolishness by gangrene."

Brant left them with the patient. He went into a lazy descent of snow from a gray sky, with hardly any wind to flutter it. The rays of street lamps, spaced distantly in this section of town, touched the fresh layer of white with a bluish radiance reminiscent of moonlight. The cold air was bracing and the stillness, broken only by the soft crunching of crystalline flakes beneath his feet, had a soothing effect. The fury of the storm had passed, leaving the semblance of peace; but in Brant's private world the chaos was only beginning.

Knowing John Macfarlane's reason for being tired of life was worse than not knowing had been. Then there had been the hope that the diagnosis would suggest the cure, but now Brant felt helpless. It was in the interpretation Mac placed upon what he believed to be facts, and in what he intended to do about them, that the situation became dreadful. Being the kind of man he was, Mac was characteristically logical in his conclusions.

Before he was fifty the most zestful part of his life was over. The hard-fisted fighting which had been meat and drink to him came to an end with the solid establishment of the Red Rock Paper Company. There was nothing for him to do but settle down to an even tenor of existence only slightly complicated by the comparatively simple problems of managing his employees and producing and selling his product.

He might have become accustomed to easy prosperity and grown old gracefully had not his first wife, his companion of twenty-five years, died. Then, as loneliness closed in upon him and he needed all his strength to keep going, Ella Morgan came to Red Rock. Although only half his age, she had a maturity of viewpoint equal to his own and a gay gallantry that was infectious. As his secretary she won his respect and friendship at the very outset, and when having watched the widening rift between Ella and Brant and concluded that nothing would bridge or close it—Mac had bashfully proposed marriage, her acceptance of him as a husband had changed him entirely. It had rejuvenated him, tapped his generous heart and loosed such a flood of unselfish devotion as few women are privileged to receive.

And it was for her that he wanted to step out of the picture, efface himself utterly, now that he had come to believe her happiness lay elsewhere. Because he could see no point in living without her, and dreaded a return to the loneliness in which she had found him—and because if he lived he might become involved in criminal proceedings that would frighten and hurt her—he intended, quite reasonably, to die.

Brant turned the corner into Superior Street, his jaw clenched in bitterness. Ahead of him glowed the red-and-yellow sign of the Idle Hour Theater. The ticket booth was dark, which meant that the last show was well under way. He read the scarlet letters on the posters—*Down Among the Dead Men*—and wondered how many of the townsfolk had gone there like Carol with the idea that fictional murder would rinse the taste of the real thing out of their mouths. Not many, he guessed; the snow was still bad enough to keep most people at home after nightfall.

Then, as he passed the theater and came abreast of the Apex Grocery next door, he heard a grunting and a scuffling. Halting, he peered into the darkness of the tunnel that led to the door of the store, which was closed for the night. His eyes made out a bulky shape bending over, swaying a trifle.

"Hey!" he said experimentally.

The shape whirled and the white blob of a face appeared. There was another smaller shape beside the large one; it slumped to the floor Of the tunnel. More by intuition than recognition Brant knew that Al Nowka, the liquor-crazed Pole, was in there and that he had been struggling with another person.

An instant later there was a gasp and a strangled voice crying, "Help!"—and the voice was Carol's.

Brant moved without conscious thought, springing toward the tunnel, and Nowka lunged forth to meet him. Boxing had been one of Brant's interests in college and he had not neglected it since; he dodged a murderous sweep

of Nowka's fist and drove his knuckles hard against the big
fellow's chest and chin.

It was like punching a padded statue. Nowka paid no
attention to the blows, but aimed a powerful one of his
own that Brant failed to duck. It seemed to Brant that a
pile-driver had rammed the side of his head; before he realized that he was falling he struck the snow-covered earth
sidewise.

He was up instantly, shaking his head to clear it, hitting desperately. There was no need for skill in this bout,
for Nowka made no pretense of keeping a guard. He simply
slugged, grunting each time one of his long arms lashed
out.

Behind Nowka, Carol was on her feet, tugging at his
coat and screaming. Brant wanted to warn her to keep
away, to run for safety, for he knew he could not hope to
win the fight, but he had no spare breath to speak with.

A glancing blow across the temple made flashing lights
dance before his eyes, so that he did not see the knockout punch coming. It caught him squarely on the tip of
the chin, lifted him clear of the ground and hurled him
backward. He could have sworn that his shoulders hit the
street before his hips did.

There was no blackout. Total unconsciousness would
have been preferable, however, to the paralysis that took
possession of his body. He lay on his back, quivering in all
his limbs, unable to move; but his mind was unfogged and
his eyes missed nothing. He was aware even of the tranquil
caresses of the falling snow on his face.

He saw Nowka come forward and lift a huge foot to
smash it down in his face—a leather-booted foot that
would leave him marred for the rest of his life if it did not
kill him. He saw Carol pulling at Nowka's arm, making no
more impression than a gnat would make on a hippopotamus.

He noticed the jagged tear from collar to skirt of her blue-and-white jacket.

He tried to close his eyes, and could not. . . .

Suddenly there were shouts and running footsteps. Nowka's boot stamped down, but he was swinging ponderously to face a new enemy and the heel missed Brant's cheek by the fraction of an inch. A deep familiar voice bellowed, "You're under arrest, Nowka!" and added a torrent of practiced profanity.

Into Brant's vision flashed the broad figure of Sheriff Ed Worth and the gangling frame of Ray Saunders, his deputy.

Nowka was not in a mood to surrender gracefully. He launched a blow at Worth, who stooped and let the fist whizz harmlessly over his head. Unlike Brant, Worth made no attempt to use his hands; he swung his right foot upward and sidewise, pivoting on the other foot much as figure skater makes a sharp turn on a single blade. The toe of his boot caught Nowka low in the belly and the man bent double with a hoarse cry and fell on his side.

"Put the cuffs on him, Ray," Worth said. He looked at Carol. "You hurt?"

"N-no. I guess not. Andy came just in time. He was choking me."

"Been hunting him for two hours. Reckon it'll be a long time before he gets out of jail. . . . Say, is Andy knocked out?"

"He took a terrible beating."

She spoke from close beside Brant, being suddenly on her knees there. She had his head cradled in her arms against her breasts. Then her lips were against his, soft and frantic, and her tears were falling on his face as lightly as the snowflakes had fallen there.

"Oh, my darling, what did he do to you? Oh, Andy, my dear!"

13

Ed Worth came into the Northland Cafe as Brant was finishing his breakfast of wheat cakes and sausages. The sheriff edged into the booth, waving Lola Tucker away when
she came to ask for his order.

"Nice morning, Andy. Any bad effects from the ruckus
last night?"

The younger man shook his head. His jaw and the left
side of his skull ached and there were numerous bruised
spots about his body, but the matters that gave him genuine concern could not be blamed on Al Nowka.

"I got some investigating to do about Charlie King and
maybe Crane," said Worth. "You been around and seen
how the city police operate and you could give me some
pointers. How about coming along?"

"Glad to," Brant agreed, not a bit deceived. Worth
wanted his company because he suspected Brant of knowing more than he had told, and hoped to learn indirectly
what he could not find out otherwise. Still it would be
interesting and perhaps profitable to observe the sheriff
at work.

"Reckon we better take a look at King's room first.
Should of done it yesterday, but a lot of things come up in
the afternoon and Nowka kept me busy all evening."

"Did Nowka say anything?"

"He was too drunk last night. He went to sleep after he'd tired himself out trying to break down the jail. This morning he's too sick to talk. I gave him one drink, but it didn't do much good and I didn't know that I ought to give him any more after the way he acted."

"If he killed Charlie how are you going to prove it?"

"No way, unless we can find a witness. Maybe I'm dumb when it comes to detective work, but I can't find a single clue. Al is going to serve time, though. Lola can hardly wait to testify against him. A man can get up to twenty years for attempted rape." He coughed. "There won't be no need for Carol to testify. I don't reckon she'll want to, and it would be better to leave her out of it."

Outside, the snow had dwindled to a fine haze that sifted down unobtrusively, not aggravating the condition of the streets to any noticeable degree. They walked to the Hotel Alger, taking a route that did not bring them past the Macfarlane house. The hotel was a sprawling frame building in need of paint, dignified only by the cracked sign above its porch, which bore in addition to the name the legend, *"Rooms $2 Wk"* It was run by Emma Jorgensen, a lean and forbidding woman, who listened without comment to Worth's explanation of his visit. When he had finished, she marched upstairs ahead of them, unlocked a room on the second floor and left without having spoken a word or permitted a shade of expression to disturb the impassivity of her countenance.

"Ten minutes will get us out of here," Brant said, looking curiously about the cheerless room, which was so small that a single bed, a varnished dresser and a straight chair made it appear crowded. There was a round rug in the center of the floor, an illustrated last year's calendar against the cracked plaster of a wall with a narrow window. A cardboard suitcase had been stowed under the bed and a shallow closet without a door contained articles of clothing.

"Don't know as I blame Charlie for getting drunk every chance," Worth muttered. "Imagine having to come home to a dump like this."

"He made decent money at the mill. He could have had a better place. He drank because he didn't have sense enough to do anything else."

"That's another good reason." Worth started pawing through the drawers of the dresser. He drew from beneath a pile of dirty clothing a quart vinegar bottle filled with pale yellow fluid and stoppered with a whittled cork. He sniffed of the contents. "Moonshine

from Maggie Tucker's. Smell's worse'n any other brand in the county."

Brant investigated the pockets of the clothing in the closet without finding anything of importance. He opened the suitcase, which contained a pair of rubber boots and a moth-eaten suit of flannel underwear. He turned back the carpet, then stood beside the sheriff and looked at the contents of the dresser as they were sorted over. The most interesting discovery was an old model .32 caliber five-shot revolver, rusted where the nickel had been worn from its barrel; it was unloaded and there were no cartridges to be found, and Worth asserted it had not been fired in years.

Nowhere was there a letter, magazine or newspaper, or anything on which words were printed or written. Brant remarked about it.

"Charlie never went to school," Worth explained. "He could figure money as quick as you or me, but he couldn't read nor write nor even sign his name."

A minute later Worth rolled back the mattress from the bedsprings and uncovered a scarlet hunting cap and one expensive mitten lined with fur.

"Crane's," said Brant.

"Reckon that comes pretty close to proving something, Andy. Crane wouldn't be shedding his clothes in the kind of weather we been having if he was alive and in his right mind."

"He left those things on the floor of the paper mill night before last, Ed. I was there and saw them. King came in for a few minutes and when he left I noticed they were gone."

The sheriff asked sharply, "Was Mac in the mill then?"

"That isn't the point. Did you hear what happened to Jim Scott?"

"Nope. It's funny how an officer of the law is apt to be the last man in town to hear of things. What about Scott?"

"He worked that night and when he was ready to go home in the morning he couldn't find his cap and one of his mittens. They'd been stolen from his locker. Crane was the only person who would need them, but he couldn't have stolen them if he'd been dead."

"Mac was there, wasn't he?" Worth persisted.

"Yes, but what has that got to do with it?"

"Plenty, maybe. Mac is nobody's fool. If he killed Crane—and mind you I'm not saying he did or that he wasn't justified if he did—he'd know about the cap and mitt. Suppose he was going to get rid of them, but King got to them first. What would be the smartest thing Mac could do?" He answered his own question. "Swipe somebody else's cap and mitt so people would think Crane had swiped them and couldn't be dead!"

Brant was dismayed. It was a logical deduction, but, it had never occurred to him. Of course, Mac had not done that; nevertheless the mere suggestion that he could have made the outlook darker.

"The body—" he began.

"You know as well as me what could happen to the body. There's a sluice that runs from the lake in under the mill to float logs, and Crane could be there under two or three feet of ice. There's the pulp vats, and he could be in one of them eaten up by acid."

"What if Crane was alive, but wanted it thought he was dead, and Charlie King knew he was alive? That would give Crane a motive for choking Charlie to death."

Worth retorted, "What if Crane was dead and King knew that? King would have a motive for trying to get money from Mac and shooting Mac when there was an argument—because Mac never did shoot himself like he says. Then Mac would have a motive for chasing Charlie outside and choking him before he bled so much he passed out."

Once more Brant found himself respecting Worth's shrewdness. "Mac didn't kill King," he declared. "I asked him point blank and he told me he didn't. That may sound simple, but Mac trusts me to the limit and he'd have told me the truth no matter what it was."

"I hope you're right. Nobody thinks more of Mac than I do. If I wasn't the sheriff I wouldn't give a damn if he killed a man like Crane or King every day, but since I ran for election and won I got to stand by the law. I get pretty sick of my job sometimes." A note of plaintiveness crept into his voice. "Besides, if I don't solve this case somebody else will, and the chances are the guilty man will land in prison whether we like it or not. They're opening the highways, trains will be running in a day or two, and any minute the state police will start patrolling again. Those cops know their business. If they find an unsolved murder here they won't waste any time going to work."

"I know it," Brant said, "and I'm with you. Only I think when the truth comes out, if it does, it will leave Mac with clean hands."

"I hope you're right," Worth repeated.

They went back to the Northland Hotel and roused Eric Nordquist out of his chair in the lobby. He rubbed his eyes and shuffled in his fleece-lined moccasins to the desk, where he produced a flat key from a pigeonhole.

"Crane's room, eh? Then he ain't coming back, Ed?"

"Couldn't say about that, Eric, but if he didn't come back yet it looks doubtful."

Nordquist preceded them up the stairs. At the door of the room next to Brant's he stooped to examine the padlock.

"Nobody touched it. Rigby ain't been snooping any more. You was the last one inside, Andy."

"How about you when you put on the lock?"

"I didn't go in. I'm a man that minds his own business. I ain't been near the place since."

Brant stepped into the room as the door opened. The first thing he saw was the film of talcum powder across the top of the dresser where Rigby had upset the tin, and in the center of it the plain print of a huge hand. He looked over his shoulder at Nordquist.

"You wouldn't fool me?"

"No." Nordquist noticed the print. "If that's what you mean it must of been made by somebody else."

The hand that had left its outline in the powder was distinctive. There were the marks of the thumb, the index finger and the little finger, and a single broad mark where the two middle fingers should have been. Fingers webbed together as Nordquist's were would have left just such an impression.

"I don't know anybody else with hands like that," said Brant.

Worth was staring at the dresser. He said, "Come here, Eric." He grabbed the man's right hand and pressed it into the powder beside the print.

The two outlines were identical.

"Must of been before the storm when I was here to see about the window being broke," Nordquist mumbled, rubbing the white stuff from his hand on his trousers.

"It couldn't have been," said Brant. "That powder was spilled by Rigby when I surprised him yesterday." He pulled out the drawer in which was the packet of letters, and it was apparent that someone had been rummaging there since he had last closed it. The packet was no longer held intact by a rubber band and the papers were scattered. "What did you take, Eric?"

"I wasn't here," the hotel owner protested stubbornly.

Worth said, "No sense in lying when the proof's against you."

"I ain't lying." Nordquist's eyes were lowered. "I wasn't in this room, not for a week or more. I never touched a thing."

"All right," Worth sighed. "Leave us alone, Eric. If anything's missing or been tampered with we'll be seeing you."

"I mind my own business," Nordquist said, going toward the stairs.

Brant began examining the letters methodically. There were twenty or thirty of them and the first few were by no means significant except as they reflected on Crane's character. A man who signed himself "Bob" explained why he could not lend Crane the hundred dollars he had requested—*"The crap games have been cleaning me every payday and I've forgotten what it's like to have that much cash."* A girl named Molly wrote, *"Sure I'm being faithful to you— you jealous old thing—but I can't say for how long if you don't come out of the woods and pay me a visit."* He found no mention anywhere of John or Ella Macfarlane nor any hint of what troubles may have arisen in that direction.

He did find, however, halfway through the letters, an envelope with a Detroit postmark, mailed within the week and addressed in the same tight, angular scrawl that distinguished Peter Rigby's signature in the register downstairs. He took out the sheet of paper it held, unfolded it and read:

*Dear Ralston: Will arrive Thursday with badge
and warrant mentioning 10 grand, as per your
directions. Make sure everything is set.*

Pete

"Here we are," he said. "I'll bet a shiny dime this is
what Rigby was after. It puts the whole business in a different light."

Worth read the note. "Reckon there was a mite of
skullduggery afoot. Ten thousand dollars' worth, anyhow.
Blackmail, do you think, Andy?"

"More than likely. And where in Red Rock could they
have hoped to collect that much, except from Mac? Only
there was a hitch somewhere, I imagine, and Crane ducked.
He might have been afraid of Mac or afraid of the law in
case the truth got out, or he might have wanted Mac to
think he was murdered."

"Or else," Worth put in dryly, "Mac lost his temper and
committed murder—or justifiable homicide—when Crane
tried to collect. If it was that way, and Mac would claim
he acted in self-defense, he could be acquitted."

Brant frowned. "Lay off Mac. Now that we've got something tangible to go on, let's get going. Why not collar
Rigby and make him come clean?"

"Not just yet. I don't say all your gabbing hasn't influenced me. Like you think, Crane could be alive and sassy,
and if he is the most likely place to look for him is Maggie
Tucker's. I didn't do a good job of looking last time I was
there and I been thinking it wouldn't hurt to go back.

"I got another reason for wanting to go there. Doc
Sperry says King was drinking heavy before he got killed.
I was at Eckstrom's and Oliphant's and every other place
where he could of got drunk, but they didn't see him. So
I reckon, unless he got drunk by himself in his room, he
was at Maggie's.

"Rigby can't get out of town. He's just as safe as if I had him in jail with Nowka, maybe safer. The more we can find out before we collar him the more we're apt to find out from him."

"You're talking sense. Let's go."

"Now hold on. There's two ways of doing anything and one of 'em is always better'n the other. If you and me walk over to Maggie's now we'll find everything neat and tidy and nothing the least bit suspicious, because somebody'll spot us two blocks off. But if we give her a surprise raid it might be a different story."

"After dark, you mean?"

"That's right. This'll be Saturday night and she'll have a gang there, swilling rotgut and raising hell. Maggie'll likely be too drunk herself to think fast. You meet me at the courthouse at about eleven o'clock. We'll take Ray Saunders along and see if we can't stir up some excitement."

"I'll be there, Ed. Don't start without me."

14

Ben Cramer was taking an order over the telephone when Brant wandered into the redolent gloom of the drug store to replenish his supply of tobacco. Surprised and pleased at this evidence of returning normalcy, Brant leaned his elbow on the glass cigar case and waited until the pharmacist had replaced the receiver.

"How long has that thing been working, Ben?"

Cramer jotted a note on a pad fastened to the wall beside the telephone. "Since early this morning. Most of the local lines are fixed, but no outside lines. Merton Case ran the Snogo ten miles out the Marquette highway last night and he says the overhead wires and a lot of the poles are down all along the way."

Brant went to the telephone, inserted a nickel in the slot and called the Macfarlanes' number. Ella answered, her voice sounding deathly tired.

"Ella, this is Andy. How is Mac?"

"All right, I guess—now. Agnes Sperry is with him."

"Did you get any sleep?"

"Hardly any. He went out around midnight and I couldn't sleep after that."

"He *what?* Did you say he went out?"

"Will you come over, Andy? I can't talk like this."

He said, "I'm starting." He appreciated her reluctance to discuss Mac by wire. Fanny Wight, the operator, was not only an inveterate eavesdropper but also an indefatigable broadcaster of whatever personal items came her way.

Ella was waiting. She admitted Brant before he could ring and held her finger to her lips, closing the door without a sound. Beckoning him to follow, she tiptoed into the kitchen, closed the doors of that room and sat at the table, resting her arms on its scrubbed maple surface. These last two days had aged her incredibly. He could not bear to see her so pitifully worn and shaken.

"He should know better than to worry you this way!" Brant said.

"Don't blame him. Whatever he was trying to do he thought was for the best. He wasn't thinking of himself."

"Did he really go outside?"

"Yes, with a revolver."

He sat down opposite her, his eyes somber. "Where did he go?"

"I don't know. He pretended to sleep after the doctor left. I lay down on the sofa about eleven and dropped off immediately, sure he would be all right. Then an hour later I awoke. The door was open and the room was freezing. I got up to close the door, thinking it had come open by itself, and saw Mac out in front. He was leaning against the snow piled beside the walk. He had blankets wrapped around him and his boots on. He had a revolver in his hand, the same one he shot himself with—if he shot himself."

"Good Lord, Ella!"

"I ran out and grabbed his arm. He came in without a word. He had to lean on me to reach the bed. I got his boots off and covered him up and put hot water bottles at his feet and rubbed his wrists. I was afraid he'd get pneumonia, but I couldn't call the doctor because the phone wasn't working and I didn't dare leave him.

"The doctor had given him two pills, but Mac had only pretended to take them. I found them under his pillow. He was so weak I was afraid to give him both of them, but I made him take one and he went to sleep in a few minutes. I sat beside him the rest of the night in case he should wake up and try to go out again."

"You poor kid! Didn't he offer an explanation?"

"He wasn't in any shape to talk. I didn't ask questions. He might have gone out just before I woke up, or nearly an hour sooner. He was covered with snow, but five minutes would have been long enough for that and long enough to make the room as cold as it was. On the other hand, if he'd been out in the street his tracks would have been covered in about the same time."

"Where could he go at that hour?"

"Oh, Andy, I—I think he was going to kill himself!"

It was the obvious conclusion to draw. Mac would not have shot himself in the house with Ella alone there, for fear of the effect upon her. He would have gone outside, taking it for granted that she would sleep until morning and not miss him until other people were around, and that by the time his body was found she would have partially reconciled herself to the idea of his death.

He said slowly, "It's fantastic to think of the Mac we know ending things that way. Still, he's been talking about dying, about wanting to die, and there could only be one other reason for his taking the revolver. . . ."

"To kill someone else," she whispered.

That was what he had meant, but it was no easier to believe than the suicide theory.

"What did he do with the gun? I'd like to see it."

"I hid it in the sofa cushions." She left the kitchen stealthily and came back with the big blue revolver dangling from her fingers at arm's length. "I hate it," she said. "It's the cause of all this."

"No," Brant replied. "They don't point and fire themselves." He swung out the cylinder and saw two spent cartridges, their copper detonation caps dented by the firing pin. He felt sure they were the same cartridges that had been discharged in Mac's office Thursday night and that the weapon had not been fired since.

"What is it?" Ella asked.

"He didn't shoot anybody." He got a dish towel from the rack near the sink and wiped the metal parts of the gun and the scored rubber grips, erasing Ella's fingerprints and his own and Mac's. In so doing he had no definite purpose, but only the uneasy thought that it might complicate matters if the state police should check the gun and find those prints. Then wrapping the revolver in the towel, he took it into the pantry and placed it on the highest shelf, a foot above his head.

"What am I going to do?" she asked. "I can't just let things slide. Today or tomorrow or next day he'll find a way to carry out whatever plan he has, unless he can be made to change his mind."

"Did you have a chance to talk to him before he went to sleep last night?"

"For a few minutes. I said I could never be happy if he didn't get well. I said it was all nonsense about you and me ever wanting to be more than friends." She stared self-consciously at the bare table. "I told him I needed him more than I needed food and drink and sleep. And you know, Andy, I meant every word of it."

"Certainly you did." That hollow pain in his chest had nothing to do with jealousy, he told himself fiercely.

"Certainly you meant it. But he couldn't have taken you at your word if he went out after that."

"He didn't. I could tell. Oh, he smiled and held my hand and promised that everything would turn out all right and there was no need for me to worry, but it was the way he would have behaved toward a child. He thought I was lying, making some great sacrifice to cheer him up."

"He's a hard-headed man, Ella. He needs to be shown proof. If only there was another girl . . ." He slapped his knee. "My God, I'm dumb! That's the answer."

"What do you mean?"

"Why, we'll tell him I'm going to be married, Ella! I'm going to settle down and have a home and a wife and children. How could you and I ever be very important to each other under those circumstances?"

Her tired brain grappled with the idea. "It might work," she said at last, "if you can make him believe it."

"I can if he'll give me time. Let's see—she shall be a blonde—no, a redhead—and—"

At that moment Mrs. Sperry came in from the next room and sat with them. No further planning was possible. Mac was still sleeping, Agnes said, but was restless and would wake before long. She was more interested, however, in May Berger's baby, born at three A.M., a seventh daughter weighing seven pounds. All the details of the birth which she had been able to glean from the doctor, when he reeled home in a state of complete exhaustion at four, came glibly from her lips. It had been a difficult forceps case—and wasn't it odd that women who had the most trouble so often had the most babies too?

Mac rumbled, "Babies be damned! What did you do with my cigars, and can't I even have water to drink?"

Ella said, "He's feeling better." She went into the next room and Brant heard the wounded man murmur, "I'm sorry I woke you up last night. I just wanted a breath of air."

Brant joined them. "Have a good rest, Mac?"

"Hello, Andy. Anything new?"

"One or two things."

"Then kick these women out of here and tell me. All I know is what I read in the *Reporter,* which doesn't print the half of it, and what I overhear Agnes telling Ella." He said thoughtfully, "There were never any babies in my house, but from what I hear it must be interesting having them."

"A pity you couldn't have one," said Agnes, who had brought ice water from the kitchen. "You men wouldn't be so quick to make a joke of it if you knew what it was like."

"Right now a baby would be too much for me. Hand me the cigars, Agnes, and put Ella to bed, will I you? I've been keeping her up day and night and she needs rest. Give her one of those dynamite pills your husband left for me."

He signaled to Brant to close the doors behind the women, and asked, "What does Ella think I was up to last night?"

"She thinks you were trying to kill yourself. What were you up to?"

Mac did not answer.

"It looked bad, your having that gun."

Mac ignored the implication. "What's doing?"

"Ed Worth and I have been looking into things. We think maybe we can rout Crane out of his hole tonight."

"Don't you go spoiling my latest batch of pulp."

"No danger. We found out that Crane and this man Rigby were in cahoots." He told about the note found in Crane's room. "They had a scheme to get money the easy way. Your money."

"Hmmm." Mac was thoughtful. "And where do you think you'll find Crane?"

"We're going to try Maggie Tucker's. Crane hung out there sometimes."

"You and Ed going there tonight?"

"That's it."

"Don't be disappointed if you don't find him. Something tells me we guessed right about him the first time."

"You're a pessimist."

"I'm a realist. You will be too when you grow up. What's Ed going to do about Rigby?"

"Nothing for the present. So far as we know he hasn't committed any crime."

"Do me a favor and keep Ed from pestering him."

Brant was amazed. "What do you care whether he's pestered?"

"I do care. I can't go into it, but it will make everything smoother if he's left alone for a day or so."

"Mac, you're keeping too many important things to yourself. I wish you'd tell me exactly what Rigby wanted of you and why he thought he'd get it."

The mill owner closed his eyes. "I know what I'm doing."

"I'm not so sure you do. It isn't like you not to fight."

"How can a man fight when he's flat on his back?"

"If you behave yourself you can be up in two or three days."

"Wrong again. Didn't we thresh that out yesterday?"

"We didn't thresh anything out. You were going to think matters over."

"I've thought them over."

Brant took a long breath. Now was the time to punch a hole in Mac's conception of things, and it had better be a big one.

"You care a lot about Ella, don't you?"

"Let's not go into that again," Mac pleaded wearily.

"You know how I feel. If it wasn't for you—"

"Listen, Mac—I don't want to upset you when you're sick, but there are a couple of points you'd better get straight right now. If you shouldn't pull through, you know you can count on me to do everything I can for Ella. But did you ever stop to think that maybe I couldn't do very much—that maybe I'd be marrying someone else?"

Mac's eyes opened. "You—marry someone else?"

"I didn't intend to say anything till it was over. You know how everyone razzes a man who's going to marry. I don't care for that. We're going to have a quiet ceremony and make a quick getaway, with no outsiders homing in till the honeymoon is ended. That's the way we both want it."

"You're making this up. How is it you never told me till today?"

"Why should I? Did you and Ella consult anybody when you decided to marry? After all, it isn't an illogical thing for me to do. I'm twenty-eight and I'm sick of living in hotels. I can support a wife—and I'm in love with a wonderful girl."

Mac's lips twitched. "You wouldn't take advantage of an old man, would you, because you thought it might make him feel better? I may be over-suspicious, but it strikes me that you and Ella might have invented this story with ulterior motives. If that's the case you're hurting yourselves more than you're helping me."

A gust of anger went through Brant. He wanted to yell at Mac, to shake him, to do violence in some form. "The girl I'm going to marry isn't a figment of the imagination," he said harshly. "You'd understand that if you weren't too damned obstinate for any use!"

Mac smiled, and the smile was genuine. "A local girl?"

He snapped, "Yes," without thinking.

"Who is she?"

In his desperation he thought of the one person he was sure he could depend on in any difficulty. He said, "Carol Johnson." As soon as he had said it he realized that she was the last person he should have named and was aghast at his immense stupidity.

But Mac was nodding and there was a new light in his eyes. He said, "I've known her since she was a squalling brat. She's a grand girl and I'm glad for you, son—if you're giving it to me on the level."

"Get yourself out of this bed and on your feet," Brant said miserably, "and we'll let you be best man."

"I might, at that. Bring your girl around to cheer me up, Andy, and we'll see. Bring her around this afternoon."

15

Doctor Sperry had hitched his chair close to the airtight stove in his cramped office. He wore a flannel dressing gown over his brown sweater, and at intervals he sneezed explosively.

"I've heard that doctors are like priests," Brant observed. "You can tell them anything and be sure that it won't be talked over in public. The secrets of the bedside and the consultation room are inviolable if not sacred. The Hippocratic oath is on the up and up."

The doctor sniffed, partly in disdain and partly in consequence of his cold.

"Get on with it. Cut out the alleged levity and say what you've come to say."

"This morning I heard all the gruesome details of a difficult accouchement. They left me limp and raveled. I'll never look at Mrs. Berger again without a sneaking sense of shame because I know things I ought never to know about her internal structure."

A chuckle escaped the physician. "Having a baby of her own never satisfied Agnes' curiosity. She's got to know about every childbirth in town, and she waits till I'm dead for sleep and defenseless and then pumps me. Most women are that way. Half the chatter over bridge tables is about having babies. In a way you can't blame 'em; it's the most important thing in their lives."

"What other cases does Agnes pump you about?"

"Sometimes she fishes for news of my patients' sex problems. But babies is her specialty. Unless you're going to have one, you can talk freely."

"It's a ticklish subject—"

"Damn it, go over and tell it to Father Kelly if you'd rather!"

"It's about Mac."

"What about him?"

Brant said slowly, "He has an idea there's something between Ella and me."

Sperry started to chuckle again, but ended by sneezing. "That's not news."

"Do you mean to say you knew it?"

"Agnes told me, but I'd have guessed it anyway. It's a matter of elementary psychology. You and Ella were in love, then you got away from each other and thought it was over. Mac thought so too, and married the girl. As a general thing it's a mistake for a middle-aged man to marry a young woman. No matter how virile he is, he looks around at the young bloods who remind him of himself twenty years ago, and begins to wonder. His wife may find him completely satisfactory, yet he can't help imagining that she's regretting his age and the limitations it puts upon him. He gets inferiority feelings and sometimes they play hell with him."

"But Mac isn't like that, and things haven't changed since his marriage."

"Yes, they have. You've come back, as pretty and high-spirited as he was twenty-five years ago. Ella talks of you and it's no secret that you'd swim Lake Superior to rescue her handkerchief if the wind happened to blow it that way."

"Damn it, that's all over. We're not in love."

"You might as well be as far as Mac is concerned. He thinks you are."

"Is that why he isn't keen about getting well?"

"That's why he tried to kill himself last night. He must have been going to, you know."

"Doc, if you knew all this, why did you ask me to find out what was wrong with him?"

"I—I—" Sperry sneezed and swore. "I wanted you to find out for yourself. There was nothing I could do about it, but I figured you might do something."

"What?"

The doctor shrugged. "You tell me."

"Well, this morning I think perhaps I made him decide to get well."

"Now you're telling me what I want to hear."

"I asked him to be best man at my wedding."

"Was it your idea or Ella's?"

"We started to talk it over together. I was going to invent a mythical sweetheart somewhere, but I got caught unprepared and I finally said I was going to be married here in town."

"What name did you give?"

Brant stared at the stove and squirmed. "Don't breathe a word about it. I mentioned Carol Johnson."

"Does she know?"

"Not yet."

"I snipped out Carol's tonsils. I brought her through the flu last winter. If I were your doctor I couldn't do better than prescribe her for you. Why not marry her?"

"She isn't—" He was going to say she wasn't in love with him, but he could not say it honestly. "I don't intend to marry anyone," he said stiffly. "All I want is your advice on how far we'll have to carry this thing."

"You'll have to keep up the pretense till Mac is completely well. That may take two or three weeks. He has a will that could move mountains—not one man in a thousand could have done what he did last night on sheer will power. But that bullet hurt him bad."

"Do you actually think he'll die otherwise?"

"He'll die if he hangs onto the idea that the only decent thing he can do is set his wife free and the only decent way he can do it is make her a widow. That man's capacity for self-sacrifice is colossal, and the same will power that can save him can kill him."

"That's all I wanted to know."

"One thing more, Andy. You may be able to save his life by pretending, but if you want to save his friendship you'd better start making love to Carol in earnest. You could hunt for a wife till you were too old to make it worth while and not find a better one."

"I'll start thinking of future troubles when present ones are out of the way. Remember, Doc—you and Father Kelly and the Sphinx are three of a kind."

Brant went into the Northland Cafe, where there was a phone booth. Lola was in a happier frame of mind today, possibly because of Nowka's arrest. She said, "How's life treating you?"

"It's all work and no play."

"Come along with Glenn and me tonight, why don't you? We're going to the Pine Tree Inn to dance and drink beer. Glenn's borrowing a car. Can you get a girl?"

"I could get a million, Lola, but I have other things to do. You and Glenn have a good time by yourselves."

The Pine Tree Inn was a roadhouse three or four miles out of town, where on Saturday nights an orchestra of sorts played for dancing. He was glad that Lola would be there during the raid on her mother's home.

He telephoned the Johnson home and learned from Mrs. Johnson that Carol had gone out to buy groceries. He ordered a cup of coffee and sat at the counter, dreading the task before him.

Lola asked, "You going to print anything about Nowka being pinched?"

"We'll put out a bulletin or an extra edition on Monday, most likely. I'll mention it, don't worry."

"You can say that I'll testify," the halfbreed girl said, her black eyes flaming. "That ape is going to get all that's coming to him."

"I hope so," he said, and left. He had to have quiet in which to think, and he could not think with Lola in front of him.

Pacing the street between the uneven cliffs of snow, he tried to plan what he would say to Carol. He must put it up to her as a sporting proposition, get her to cooperate. She would do it—somehow he felt certain of that. But he was equally aware that it would hurt and humiliate her deeply, to have to make a game of what any woman must consider almost a vital matter. If he were in her place he would feel that he was being asked to mock at what he held sacred—and yet he would do it to save a man's life.

Carol came out of the Apex Grocery through the very tunnel into which Nowka had dragged her. She was walking unsteadily under the weight of two huge paper sacks and did not see Brant until he reached for them.

"Carry your bundles, lady?"

"Golly," she said, looking up at him as she surrendered her burden. "Golly, Andy, I was thinking of you every step I took. I was thinking how nice it would be if you should come along and lug this stuff."

"I happen to be telepathic. I was in a phone booth and a voice told me, as clearly as if it had come over the wire, that you were buying fifty—no, a hundred—pounds of canned stuff at the grocery. Then your thought waves reached me and I came to the rescue as fast as I could."

"I don't believe it. If you could read my mind you'd have run for the woods, covered with blushes."

He coughed uncomfortably. "To tell the truth, I was looking for you. I called your home and your mother said you'd gone shopping."

"Andy Brant, are you going to make me work today?"

"No. I was over to see Mac a while ago and—"

"How is he?"

"It's a queer case, Carol. He can get well if he wants to, but he doesn't seem very keen about it."

"Poor Mac! And how is Ella?"

"About as sick as he is. She hasn't had more than two or three hours' rest since he was shot."

"Do you suppose her conscience is bothering her?"

"Carol!"

"Pay no attention to me, Andy. I'm a cat." She trudged along silently, wearing in place of the jacket Nowka had torn a gray coat with a white fur collar which made a soft frame for her boyish face.

As they drew near the *Reporter* office he inquired, "Are you in a hurry to get home with this stuff?"

"My folks aren't exactly starving. Why?"

"Come inside for a minute. I want to ask you something."

"Inside?" she asked faintly. "Why . . . all right."

He gave her one of the bags to carry so that he could get the key from his pocket. It was cold in the office and only a very little gray light seeped in through the tops of the windows where the snow had settled a few inches. He did not turn on a light, however; he preferred the semi-darkness for what he had to do.

"Sit down, Scoop." He placed the bags on his desk. "I've been doing a lot of thinking today and considerable talking. At Mac's I said some things I had no business saying. They just popped out."

"You're getting as bad as me," she said soberly.

"I said something about you."

"Whatever it was, I'll back it up if you say so."

It was harder going than he had anticipated. He took off a mitten and fiddled with the buttons of his coat.

"I wish you would. It's terribly important. But if you don't feel that you want to . . ."

"What did you say, Andy?"

He blurted, "I said—I said you and I were going to be married."

"Oh," she said with a catch in her voice. "Oh."

"It came out just like that. As soon as I'd spoken the words I knew I should have seen you first. That's why I was looking for you, to try to explain—"

"Andy!" She was out of her chair and standing in front of him, touching his arm timidly. "Andy, there's no need to explain. I'm dying to be your wife. If you didn't know it already it was because you were blind."

He looked into her upturned face with a kind of horror. What had he said to bring about this incredible situation? Where had he fumbled?

"But you don't understand, Carol! You wouldn't want me for a husband if you knew. I'm a fool and a—a bungler."

Her eyes shone steadily in the dusk. She held tightly to both his arms and swayed toward him.

"I know what you are. I knew when I was sixteen and you were a grown man, and I couldn't pass you on the street without blushing. Don't tell me anything more. Put your arms around me and kiss me."

His hands closed upon her shoulders. He was not sure whether he wanted to hold her close or hurl her away across the room, but he knew what he must do. They were trapped; he had trapped himself and trapped her with him; and no matter what happened he could never let her know how horribly she had been tricked and cheated in a way he had never intended.

He groaned, "You poor darling!" and held her against his chest. Her lifted lips were imperious; they commanded his mouth and gave the fury that was in him an outlet in savage kisses. Her yielding trustfulness inspired him with beautiful thoughts and thoughts that were shameful, and they churned together in his brain until, with a great effort, he pushed her away to the length of his arms.

Brant hated himself as he had never hated before. He said, "I have to go back to see Mac. If I carry your packages home first, will you go with me?"

"Do you have to ask, Andy? I'll go anywhere with you—everywhere—always."

16

Red Rock was a man's town that Saturday night. The entire male population of the county and bordering areas seemed to have assembled from the mills, lumber camps, fisheries and lonely farms, urged by a holiday mood. The men had come across country on snowshoes and skis from as far as fifteen or twenty miles, and by bus and truck and flivver over such roads as had been opened. They came in overalls and workclothes and some in mail order suits that were kept in reserve for purposes of celebration. They had money crackling and jingling in their pockets and they spent it in the stores and the saloons.

Superior Street hummed and glittered. All the shops were open and the snow had been removed from their windows so that their lights streamed out, more brilliant than the outdoor lamps. In the street people moved back and forth and lingered in groups. A lumberjack sprawled among booted feet, snoring, and down toward the Northland there was a fight. Over the entire scene played a medley of spirited sound compounded of human voices, slamming doors, mechanical pianos and juke boxes, and radios tuned to many stations.

Ordinarily such a spectacle would have delighted Brant. Tonight, however, he had no heart for frivolity, no wish to speak to people or be spoken to.

He turned the nearest corner and went away from the noise and brightness, south on Fletcher Avenue to Court Street and west a block to where the courthouse stood in the center of its unprepossessing park. He walked swiftly, swinging his arms, digging his heels into the packed snow with emphasis.

He had reached a fork in his thinking. Two paths of action branched out before him. Both led to hell.

The smoother path went by way of the marriage altar. He could marry Carol and avoid much explanation, and in the bargain win a better wife than he deserved, loyal and unselfish and responsive. He could fool her for months or years. . . . But what right had he to marry a girl like Carol under false pretenses? Why should he promise her something fine and beautiful and give her instead a shabby and sordid imitation? There would be the inevitable day of reckoning when he would stand revealed as a cheat and a betrayer and she would be crushed by shame and heartbreak.

The braver way would be to tell her the truth, however terribly it might hurt her; to beg for her understanding and forgiveness. . . . But remembering her wet and shining eyes, and later the joy that rang in her laughter, he knew he would sooner commit murder in cold blood than strike that blow.

When he had taken Carol to visit Mac and Ella that afternoon, the wounded man had looked at her and known immediately that she was not a party to any deception. He had changed before their eyes, growing confident and cheerful and even somewhat ribald, bringing hot blushes to Carol's cheeks with his talk. He swore he would be not only best man at their wedding, but godfather at all the ensuing christenings.

Whatever else he had to face, Mac knew he would not have to face the loss of Ella, and so he was not going to die. . . .

There were lights in the sheriff's office in the north wing of the courthouse. Entering the drab room Brant found Ray Saunders, the chief deputy, dozing in a chair with his feet on a desk. Saunders was a long thin man in his early thirties, with a narrow face distinguished by a drooping mustache; he opened a melancholy eye when he heard Brant's footsteps.

"Howdy, Andy. What's it like up town?"

"Like a wild west movie. You and Ed ought to be there keeping the boys in line. You could fill your jail in half an hour."

Saunders shrugged. "Where's the good in that? The last few days have been tough on those boys and they got a right to raise the devil. Them that gets their heads busted usually has it coming, and if any damage is done in the saloons they're making the money to pay for it."

"Where is Ed?"

"Downstairs tucking Nowka in for the night. Took him down half a tumbler of rye. Ed always feels sorry for anyone he has to lock up."

"Does he expect trouble at Maggie's?"

"No more'n the three of us can take care of," said Saunders complacently.

Worth came up the stairs from the basement jail. His voluminous mackinaw was buttoned and his fur hat pulled over his ears and his eyes were glinting.

"You fellers ready to start?" he asked.

They went back through Court Street the way Brant had come, speaking little. Battlements of snow rose higher than their heads at either side, effectively concealing them. Now and then they could hear a faint shout or a strain of music from Superior Street, two blocks away.

"Got a good mind to get drunk myself when this is over," muttered Saunders.

As they reached the corner of Mill Avenue sounds of revelry from another direction came to their ears—three or four voices bawling *Roll Out the Barrel* to the feeble accompaniment of a scratchy radio. The source was a small unpainted house at their right, standing by itself in the middle of the block, nearly lost in a gigantic drift. The upper half of one window was visible and yellow lamplight made a sketchy pattern of the cracks in the drawn blind behind the pane.

Worth outlined his strategy curtly. "No noise. No knocking and waiting for the door to open. We bust right in. If anybody looks like they want to fight, hit 'em first and hit 'em hard."

A path of sorts led to the front door and there was no porch to echo the sounds of their approach. The barrel song had come to an end, but the radio was carrying on with another melody and a man was laughing uproariously. The raiders had at least the advantage of surprise.

Worth went ahead of the others. The front door of the house was not locked; he turned the knob and pushed it open and strode without hesitation into the room beyond, with Brant and Saunders close behind him.

The laughter and voices ceased. The only sound was of a girl's nasal voice wailing through the radio, *"There I go, leading with my heart again . . ."*

Five men, lumberjacks from one of the camps, sat around a gallon jug of white whiskey in the center of a table covered with peeling linoleum. In a corner of the squalid room beside the flat-topped stove Maggie Tucker sat in a low rocker, staring at the newcomers balefully out of jet-black eyes.

Worth said, "'Evening, Maggie. We wanted to look around some. Don't mind, I hope?"

He had a flashlight in his hand and he opened the two other doors leading from the main room and sent its beam into the darkness beyond them. There was a woodshed which served as a kitchen in warm weather, and a bedroom with two unmade beds. It took the sheriff less than a minute to inspect them to his apparent satisfaction.

One of the lumberjacks, a tall and thickset man with black hair and eyebrows and whiskers, growled, "What's the idea?"

"Where is Crane, Maggie?" Worth demanded, ignoring the heckler. "We know he was here and we want him."

She said nothing, but her glare was poisonous. She was an unlovely creature, wrinkled and withered, although her age was probably not more than forty-five years. Her greasy hair, streaked with white, hung in uneven strings about a broad face the color of saddle leather; her sacklike woolen dress, basically brown, had been torn and stained until it defied description, and her enormous breasts made it bulge alarmingly.

"She's shy," Saunders said dryly. The deputy was watching the big lumberjack who had spoken. "You better be the same way, Mickey O'Reilly."

That individual shoved back his chair and got to his feet angrily. Brant was nearest the man. He said, "Sit down, you damned fool!"

"Me?" The lumberjack put forth an arm to brush Brant aside. "You think I'm a damn' fool?"

All the self-hatred and helpless rage that had been smoking within Brant burst into flame. He stepped inside the sweeping arm and drove his fist with all his strength to the bristly point of the other's chin.

Mickey O'Reilly lurched backward against the table. There was a thud and a jangle of breaking glass, and a volley of profanity as O'Reilly's four friends leaped up. Someone hit Brant behind the ear and he dropped to his hands and knees. Before he could get up again he had an amazing glimpse of Ed Worth in action. The tough little

sheriff lashed out with one foot while he pivoted on the
other, exactly as he had when he faced Nowka; the victim
of the kick, struck low in the groin, howled and collapsed.
Whirling, Worth grabbed the front of another man's coat
and jerked him close, then butted the top of his head into
the fellow's chin.

Metal flashed in the light of the oil lamp on a shelf behind the stove. Brant saw the naked blade of a clasp knife
jutting from O'Reilly's fist, striking at Worth's back.

Brant cried, "Look out, Ed!" and kicked with both feet
at the ankle which momentarily supported the lumberjack's weight. O'Reilly seemed to hang slanting in the air
for an instant. The knife fell to the floor, and then the
breath was crushed from Brant's lungs as the man's heavy
body crashed upon him.

Everything was blurred for seconds after that. Then the
whine of the radio singer's voice became audible again,
concerned this time with a South American subject. Brant
raised his head and saw that the lumberjacks had departed.

Maggie Tucker had not stirred during the fracas. She
was still in her rocker, her eyes spewing hate.

As if nothing had happened, Worth repeated his earlier
question while his fingers plucked at a tuft of thread where
a button had been ripped from his coat. "Where's Crane?"

The woman unbent so far as to utter two words in a
deep, sullen voice:

"Don't know."

The sheriff glanced at the carpet of burlap sacking on
which the table had stood. A portion of it sagged below
the level of the floor, as if boards beneath it had given way.

"Them hoodlums like to of wrecked the joint," Worth
observed blandly. "You ought to cater to a better class,
Maggie." He bent down and whipped back the burlap,
revealing a square opening where a trapdoor had caved in.
"Maybe we could find Crane down there, huh?"

"Don't know," Maggie said stubbornly.

Being already on the floor, Brant rolled to the opening. "Give me your flashlight, Ed." He thrust his head and shoulders beneath the floor and swept the light about the three-foot space between them and the bare earth.

There were no foundation walls, the house being raised on concrete blocks set at intervals of five or six feet. The deep snow walled in the shallow space completely, however, except that at the rear there was an oblong opening.

"A tunnel," Brant said, lifting his head. "I'm going to have a look."

"You want to take a gun along, Andy?"

"No." He lowered himself awkwardly and crouched on hands and knees beneath the beams that supported the floor. Followed by Worth's admonition to be careful, he crawled to the passage in the snow.

The tunnel was about two yards long. Before Brant entered it the flashlight showed him clean pine boards at the far end. The boards were those of a packing case four feet square and seven feet long, with one end knocked out. Kneeling in the cramped space, he saw that while it may have been intended as a cache for illicit liquor during the season of deep snows, it had served more recently as a makeshift shelter for a human being. Blankets, candle stubs, cigarette butts and a copy of yesterday's *Reporter* were there to prove it.

Excitement gripped Brant. Here was convincing evidence that Crane had not died in the pulp machinery. He had occupied the packing box as recently as last night, otherwise the newspaper would not be there. If anyone entertained the slightest doubt that Crane and not some other person had used the secret chamber, there would almost certainly be fingerprints to confound him.

He hurried back and reported his find to Worth.

"Reckon he waited till he was sure the storm was over, then hit for the woods," Worth said. He scowled at the woman. "That what he done, Maggie?"

Her tremendous breasts heaved as she raised and lowered her shoulders. She kept stubbornly silent.

It was Saunders who suggested that if there were one such hiding place about the house there might be another. His idea was that they should search the snow in the front and back. At least, he said, they would discover some hidden liquor. Since the gallon jug in the house was broken and its foul-smelling contents dissipated, they could do worse than obtain more evidence and arrest Maggie on a whiskey-selling charge, giving her the choice of standing trial or telling what had become of Crane.

And it was Saunders who chose the front yard as his territory, and had not sunk his mop handle in the snow twenty times before he shouted that he had made a find. Brant and Worth fought their way around the house, and when they reached him he was standing in the street, digging with his hands into the banked snow.

"Here's a hand," he said thickly, "—and an arm—and . . . Oh, my God!"

Ralston Crane had not been shredded by spinning knives, but he had met death in a manner scarcely less horrible. The three men identified the frozen body by its proportions and by the clothing in which it was dressed. The face was not available at the moment, being masked by an uneven formation of ice which extended over the top of the head.

The ice was darkly red at the base and brownish yellow on the outer surface, where Crane's blood had been thinned by the snow that shrouded him.

17

By Sunday morning the snow had ceased altogether and the sun shone for the first time in four days, turning the world into a dazzle of white. At ten, when Brant had dosed himself into full wakefulness with quantities of black coffee, the thermometer marked eighteen above zero and was climbing steadily.

There was an air of cheerfulness abroad in the town, a lessening of tension, as if mankind and the storm gods had signed a truce. Brant sensed it in all the people he had seen and spoken with in the hotel lobby and the restaurant.

The feeling was founded largely upon substantial accomplishments. During the night two locomotives had driven a snowplow through from St. Ignace, clearing the tracks. Information received at the railroad station over the newly repaired telegraph line was that a train from Marquette would arrive at twelve-thirty on its way south, and at five the train from St. Ignace would bring mail and passengers from Detroit and lower Michigan. Today or tomorrow, it was said, the principal highways would be open from Marquette to the Straits of Mackinac and the Soo, and within two or three days the lesser roads would be fit for travel and there would be no more isolated settlements in the Upper Peninsula.

The shooting of John Macfarlane and the murder of Charlie King had been talked over so thoroughly that no one had much to say about them today. It was taken for granted that Ed Worth was hopelessly baffled and nothing further could be expected of him, but that the state police would get at the truth in good time. Red Rock was willing to wait as long as need be for the story, which did not rank as of vital importance anyway, since Macfarlane was not going to die and King had been a citizen of no account.

The murder of Ralston Crane was not yet a matter of public knowledge. Simon Perrault, the undertaker and coroner, had been sworn to secrecy and was keeping the corpse hidden. It was the sheriff's thought that the apprehension of the killer would be easier if he were not forewarned by news of the discovery.

People said that Crane was a storm casualty, and one fine day in spring his body would be found at the bottom of a snowdrift.

The waitress who was taking Lola Tucker's place in the Northland Cafe gave Brant his check. He left silver on the table and got up, strolling into the lobby of the hotel. He grinned at Ray Saunders, blinking red-rimmed eyes in a chair by the window.

"No sign of him yet, Ray?"

"Why should he miss his sleep because I'm missing mine?" demanded the deputy. "I listened at his door a while back and he was sawing wood a mile a minute."

"Well, he can't sleep forever."

"Give me ten minutes, Andy," Saunders begged. "Sit down and let me shut my eyes just that long. I swear I'll pass out for good if you don't. You got nothing to do but wait for Ed."

Saunders had been stationed in the lobby at three A.M., as soon as Lola and Glenn Quarfield had been brought from the Pine Tree Inn to the courthouse. His orders were to see that Rigby did not attempt to leave town, for it appeared extremely likely that before the end of the day Worth would want to arrest the pudgy stranger for the murder of Crane. Brant and Worth had gone to bed eventually, but Saunders had remained on duty.

"Relax," Brant said, taking another chair. "Sweet dreams."

Saunders' eyes closed and his head dropped on his chest. A gentle snore issued from his nostrils.

Lighting his pipe, Brant reviewed the crowded events of the night. The finding of Crane's body had meant only one thing to him.

"Rigby killed him!" he had exclaimed, his gaze held hypnotically by the crimson-iced corpse. "He must have. They were mixed up together in that ten-thousand-dollar blackmail scheme, or whatever it was, and they must have had an argument. Maybe it had something to do with Crane's failure to meet Rigby. Maybe Crane was trying to pull off the game without Rigby and keep all the proceeds for himself."

Sheriff Worth agreed that it was probable. "But I'm not going to arrest Rigby till I'm sure. If they were after Mac's money, what would keep Mac from doing this?"

"That bullet would keep him from it. Somebody was in that packing box as late as yesterday evening, reading my paper, which didn't come out till four o'clock. That somebody was Crane, because nobody else is unaccounted for. And Mac has been in bed at home since the first night of the blizzard."

Worth drew a hand from its mitten to rub his nose. "You and Doc Sperry know how to keep your mouths shut, but Agnes Sperry never learned. In a roundabout way I heard she'd been telling her closest friends about Mac being out for a walk last night and coming back all tuckered, like he'd been taking strenuous exercise."

Brant was jolted. In the excitement he had forgotten Mac's midnight expedition. Now he remembered that Ella had said Mac might have gone out a minute or two before she awoke, or an hour earlier. He remembered too that Mac had said earlier that evening, *"If I didn't kill Crane . . . I'd do it now if I had the chance."*

Looking at the congealed blood that covered the dead man's face and skull, Brant reflected that either a bullet from a heavy caliber revolver, like Mac's, or a beating with its butt might have brought about that result.

"You'd better arrest Rigby anyway," he said.

"I'm going to get all the information there is to be had before I arrest anybody, Andy. But I'll have the hotel watched in case Rigby tries to light out."

He sent Saunders to wake up Perrault and Sperry, and then proceed to the Pine Tree Inn in search of Lola and Quarfield. Later, taking old Maggie along with them, they removed the body to Perrault's establishment on Fletcher Avenue without being seen.

As the ice turned to watery gore in the heat of Simon Perrault's stove, Sperry made a cursory examination of the dead man's head.

"Brain mashed like potatoes," the doctor pronounced graphically. "He was beaten to death. Looks like the skull was fractured in a dozen places by something round and heavy, like the head of a hammer."

"How about the butt of a revolver?" Worth inquired.

"All right, like the butt of a revolver. I might be able to tell for sure in the morning, if I don't die of overwork and exposure between now and then. Meanwhile one guess is as good as another."

"Which was it, Maggie?" The sheriff met her unwinking eyes. "Was it a hammer or a gun?"

"Don't know nothin'," she said unemotionally.

"You wouldn't like to go to prison for killing him, would you? It would be tough spending the rest of your life in a cell without liquor. . . ."

She shrugged, maintaining her fatalistic calm.

Saunders brought Lola and Quarfield to the courthouse a few minutes after Worth and Brant had disposed of Lola's mother by locking her in the little-used room reserved for female prisoners. Worth questioned the printer first, out of Lola's hearing, and sent him away after warning him not to talk about Crane. Quarfield left under protest; he had insisted he knew nothing about Crane, but he was determined not to leave Lola alone to face an official inquisition. He was escorted out of the courthouse finally by Saunders, the latter being on his way to take up his vigil at the Northland Hotel.

Lola was indignant at having her night of beer and dancing interrupted, the more so because Saunders had refused to say why Worth required their presence. While the sheriff was engaged with Quarfield she proceeded to regale Brant with a recital of her grievances.

"He'd ought to of brought a warrant if he wanted to bring us in. I know that much about the law. But he just come up to us on the dance floor and said Worth wanted us and we were to come in a hurry. Glenn tried to argue with him, but he wouldn't listen. Glenn ought to of kicked him down the stairs—and if he had I'd of gone right to court with him and testified it was Saunders' fault.

"If he'd said it was something about Al Nowka it would of been different. I'd ride a million miles on a fence rail to make trouble for that dirty Polack. But I ain't done no crime and if anybody dares to say I did I'll make it hot as the hinges of hell for them!"

"Sometimes," Brant informed her, "having knowledge of a crime and not saying anything about it is as bad as doing it yourself."

It was then that he saw the sharp fear under her indignation, in the form of a gray shadow that wriggled in her dark eyes, and knew that she could help them if she would.

When he was rid of Quarfield, Worth came to where she was sitting. "Hello, Lola," he said pleasantly. "You know what this is all about, I suppose."

"How d'you expect me to know anything? Saunders wouldn't say nothing and Andy is just as—"

"It's about Ralston Crane."

Her rouged lips parted. "How could I know anything about him?"

"He's been murdered. It happened at your place."

"Oh, my God!" she gasped. "Who done it? Where's Ma?"

"Your ma is here, locked up because she won't talk. We were going to ask you who done it."

"Me? I don't know a thing about it." Her voice rose hysterically. "You got no right to keep me here! I don't know anything, I tell you, and I want to go home!"

"There ain't nobody at your place and there was a gang of hoodlums there that about wrecked the house, so you're better off here. You might stay long enough to get to like it unless you want to tell us why Crane was staying around your ma's while everybody was hunting him."

"I don't know. I don't know anything about him. Listen, Ed Worth—and you too, Andy Brant—I never had nothing to do with Crane. He would of liked me to, but I couldn't be bothered. If you're trying to make out I killed him—"

"We ain't," said the sheriff. "We don't think neither you nor your ma done it. We think maybe we know who did. All we want is for you to tell us all you can. Do that and you won't have no trouble."

"You promise that?"

"I promise to be fair, Lola. You ought to know I always been more'n fair, pretending not to see things that maybe I'd ought to see. Why, I could have your ma in jail most of the time if I wanted to be mean, but the only time I locked her up before now was when Slim Ferguson got stabbed in her place."

She gnawed her lip, considering. "All right, I'll tell you everything I know, which ain't very much. If it helps you, all right. If it doesn't, I done the best I could. I'll go back to Thursday night when the blizzard was worst. . . ."

That night, as Brant and Worth already knew, she and Quarfield were at Oliphant's bar until about eleven-thirty, when she started home with Quarfield helping her and even carrying her where the going was hardest. On the way they saw a man near the spot where King's body was later found—a large man who appeared to be having trouble, as if he were drunk—

"Or wounded?" Worth interrupted.

She said, "It wasn't Macfarlane, if that's what you mean. It was Al Nowka. I wasn't sure at first, but after he tried to do that to me the next day I was sure. Take me to court and I'll swear to it on the Bible."

Quarfield had left her almost as soon as they reached her house. Her mother was already in bed and Lola lost no time in getting under the blankets where it was warm.

Next morning she arose and started for work at the cafe, but the snow was so bad she returned to the house for an old pair of snowshoes someone had left there. As she opened the door Crane was just emerging from the trap-door in the floor, having spent the night in the packing box under the snow.

Crane told her that he would make it worth her while not to tell of seeing him. He was going to get some money for pretending to be dead, he said, and had made arrangements with her mother to keep him hidden for a few days. He was going to give her mother five hundred dollars and he would give her the same amount for keeping the secret. So she told no one. . . .

"Not even Quarfield?" asked Brant.

"Especially not him. stupid!" said Lola. "He'd of raised hell if he knew Crane was under the same roof with me. You know how jealous Glenn is. Watches me all the time. Now he wants me to marry him."

"You could do a lot worse. Glenn Quarfield's a pretty steady guy."

"Sure, but you don't pick husbands the way you pick printers. And anyway, there's one thing I want you to understand. There was never anything happened to me with Crane that shouldn't. I didn't even see him after that first morning."

"Not Friday night when you went home?"

"No. I didn't go home till late. I was scared on account of Nowka and went to a girl friend's till I heard he was in jail. I asked Ma about Crane but she just looked at me. When Ma makes up her mind not to talk, she doesn't talk."

Worth mumbled, "You can say that again."

"On Friday I heard about Macfarlane getting shot and then King was found murdered. I was kind of scared, those things happening and Crane hiding as if he might of done 'em. I didn't know what to think, honest. So I tried not to think at all. Before long that filthy Al Nowka came in and gave me other things to think about."

"I don't reckon you got much to worry about now, Lola," Worth said. "I want you to stay here with your ma tonight, to keep her company and to make sure you won't tell about Crane. I'll turn you loose tomorrow. Does that suit you?"

It did not suit her particularly, but that was the way of it. . . .

Ed Worth came into the lobby of the Northland now, stamping the snow from his boots. He looked at Brant, bobbing his head, and then at his slumbering deputy.

"Take off his hat, Andy, and see if somebody bashed in his brains, too. Otherwise I can't figure what would make him go to sleep on an important job."

Brant said, "Have a heart, Ed. He could hardly keep his eyes open, so I said I'd spell him till you came. He's been napping about fifteen minutes and no one has been upstairs or down in that time."

"It don't look good for folks to see a peace officer sleeping in public. It gives 'em the wrong idea. We get laughed at enough when we stay awake."

"No one saw him. There's no one around. Eric Nordquist went to church and the hotel is running itself till he comes back."

Worth was mollified. "I been to see Sperry. He thinks Crane was killed late Friday night." He added, "I got the old lady talking this morning too, after working on her for an hour."

"Maggie? What did she say?"

He quoted her. She had, it seemed, broken her sullen silence long enough to apply to Worth practically every profane, obscene and indecent appellation she had heard in the course of a wicked life.

Brant laughed. "How long are you going to keep her?"

"Not a minute longer'n I got to. I run a decent jail. It's all right for the gentlemen guests to cuss me out if they feel like it—I'd do the same if I was them—but I don't like cussing women around the premises. Reckon I'll be satisfied about who the killer is in a couple hours, and have him in jail or under guard, and then I'll kick the old girl out."

"Shall we talk to Rigby now?"

"I'd rather take the hard part first. I'm going to see Mac and his missus and get the truth out of them if I have to use a crowbar. You're a good friend of theirs, so you better come along to smooth things over in case Mac lets loose that temper of his and I get mad myself."

He went up to Saunders and began shaking him.

As far as Mac and Ella were concerned, this was going to be a showdown between them and the sheriff, Brant knew. There had been two murders and there was reason to believe a major crime of another kind had been attempted, and Mac was somehow closely connected with those matters. Ed Worth had a perfect right to insist on frankness, and if Mac failed to cooperate Worth's only recourse would be to ask the state police to try where he had failed.

Brant could not believe that Mac had committed either of the murders, but neither could he dispel from his mind the possibility that he had.

Apart from that, there was the question of what had linked Ella and Crane, causing her to cry on his shoulder near Carol Johnson's house the night before the blizzard, and to meet him in the watchman's shack at the mill a few minutes before Crane and Mac fought. Whatever it was, Mac had guarded the secret fiercely and Ella had given Brant to understand that she could not divulge it because someone else was involved.

He felt that the explanation of everything might lie in that secret, and it would have to be made known before the story could be complete even if the telling were painful.

18

Ella Macfarlane opened the door to their ring and smiled brightly. "Come right in, Sheriff Ed and Editor Andy, even though the circles under your eyes prove you were roistering last night."

"I've been on pleasanter roisters," Brant said. "Your own eyes never looked better." It was true; she was fresh and animated and the look of weariness had vanished from her face. The change that had come over her since yesterday was little short of miraculous.

"Oh, we're over the worst of our troubles." She look their coats and hung them on the rack at the foot of the stairs. "Mac is healing up fast and I'm getting my beauty sleep. He's wide awake and he'll be glad to see you."

"I wonder," Worth muttered.

She noticed their seriousness for the first time. It hurt Brant to see the tightening of her lips and the flicker of anxiety in her eyes.

"You aren't bringing trouble, I hope." She looked at Brant. "You wouldn't do anything to upset him now, when he has just started on the road back? I wouldn't let you see him if—"

"Don't worry, Ella." Worth shuffled his feet in embarrassment. "We're both good friends of his. I won't pretend we came to talk about the weather, but we'll be careful not to rub him the wrong way. You can take my word for it, we got a good reason for coming."

"Trust us," Brant said. "Trust me, Ella."

Her fear was mounting. "What else has happened? I can tell it's something bad. Was there another—?"

Mac's voice cut across her whispered questions, saving them the trouble of answering. "If you don't stop talking behind my back I'll get up and knock your heads together!"

"Eavesdropping again, eh?" Brant gave Ella a glance of reassurance and went into the sickroom. "By golly, you look well enough to lick the pair of us at that. But the guy with me is Ed Worth, who gets in some fancy footwork in a fight, so you'd better pipe down."

"I've seen Ed in action, but I'd take a chance with him," Mac rumbled. He was sitting up in bed with pillows at his back and magazines and cigar ashes strewn over the rumpled spread. He looked very like his old self, gray eyes clear, cheeks and chin shaven,

hands steady. The crinkle of fine lines at the corners of his eyes showed that he was in good humor.

Worth came in with Ella. Worth said, "Besides that, I brought my gun. If a little thirty-eight slug can do this to you, one of my forty-fives would bust you clean in half."

"Not me, copper. You think I was really hurt? I was kind of lazy, that's all, and wanted an excuse to go to bed for a while."

Ella and Worth sat in chairs beside the bed and Brant leaned over Mac's feet. There was an awkward silence in which Mac stared curiously at the two men.

"Say it," he urged. "Are you going to pinch me?"

Brant flexed his hands. "We pulled that raid, Mac."

"I warned you that you'd be disappointed."

"We weren't, not entirely. We found Crane."

Mac's eyes gleamed and Ella caught her breath. Mac asked, "What did you do with him?"

"Well . . ." Brant coughed. "There wasn't much we could do except take him to Simon Perrault's. Someone killed him Friday night."

He was watching Ella as he spoke. The color fled from her face and her slim body became rigid. She would be thinking, as he was, of Mac's unexplained absence from the house that night.

"Someone beat him over the head with a hammer," Worth said, "or the butt of a revolver."

Brant could not bear Ella's terror. He said hastily, "We're pretty sure it was Rigby. We know he and Crane were up to something crooked."

"Then go after Rigby," Mac snapped, his humor changing suddenly. "Why bother with it? Neither Ella nor I have the least interest in Crane, alive or dead."

"Take it easy, Mac." Brant tightened his jaw. They were going to have this thing out now or never, and since it was an affair of life and death it was ridiculous that one man's stubbornness should stand in their way. "You know perfectly well why we're here. We can be satisfied in our own minds that Rigby is a murderer, but what we need is proof. Before we can put the story together we have to know something about Crane. You can help us there."

"What would I know about him?"

"You brought him here from Detroit. He wasn't a paper man, but you made him assistant manager. Why?"

"I refuse to discuss it."

"Is that your final word?"

"It is."

"Then," Brant said, "we've asked what we came to ask and heard what you have to say. I hope you change your mind, but whether you do or not there's no sense in arguing about it. We've been friends too long, the whole lot of us, to start squabbling over other people. Besides, the state police will take over the case and they can check on Crane through Detroit."

"Yeah," Worth mumbled, rising. "I sure hate to see them troopers come into it, but I can't stop 'em. Mac, I'm glad to see you well and kicking again. Hope our call didn't bother you none—nor you, Ella."

She said, "Sit down, Ed. Wait, Andy. I have something to say."

"Be careful," Mac warned.

"Oh, Mac. I've been careful too long. I'm not ashamed and I never was." She addressed Brant swiftly, as if she wanted to have her say before anyone could interfere. "Ralston Crane was my cousin. We were brought up together like brother and sister. That's our deep, dark secret!"

Brant looked at her blankly. He had expected that when and if the revelation came it would be dramatic, perhaps shocking. The fact that Crane and Ella were cousins might explain why she had wept on his shoulder, but how could it have caused two murders and a shooting?

He repeated pointlessly, "Your cousin."

"Not a very nice relative, either," she went on. "As far as I know he never did an honorable act in his life. However he died—whoever killed him—it's a safe bet that he had it coming."

"Ella!" said Mac.

"What's the use of stopping now?" she cried. "The worst of it is off my chest and you have no idea how much better I feel. Wouldn't you rather have me tell it than have the police get it from other sources? His record will be on file in half a dozen cities.

"My father and mother died when I was a child, as you know, Andy, and I was brought up by an aunt in Grand Rapids. She was Ralston's mother. He broke her heart and probably hastened her death. All through his 'teens he was in trouble, and as soon as he was old enough he began getting in jail. Aunt Kate spent what little money she had getting him out of his scrapes with the authorities.

"After she died he began to depend on me to save him from his creditors and the police. I was working for Mac and every few weeks I'd get a begging letter. Ralston was sick of starving, or had got into another mess and was afraid of prison. He used all the excuses. Finally I got tired of sending him money and turned him down cold."

After that she did not hear from Crane for nearly a year. But somehow he learned of her marriage to Mac, and two or three months ago Mac had a letter from him. Crane was under arrest for stealing two thousand dollars from a firm that had employed him in Detroit. He wrote that he was penitent and wanted to reform, and took care to point out that if he went to prison it would reflect undeserved disgrace upon Ella. One more chance was all he asked, for Ella's sake as much as his own.

Mac did not consult Ella, who had never mentioned Crane to him. Instead he did what he thought she would have wanted. He went to Detroit, supposedly on a business trip, and succeeded in having the charge against Crane dropped after repaying the two thousand dollars. Then, never content to do things by halves, he offered Crane a fresh start in Red Rock.

"That was where I made the mistake of my life," said John Macfarlane. "I thought I could make a man of him and Ella would be pleased. I never stopped to think that if God Almighty hadn't been able to make anything of him, I didn't stand much chance."

Mac made one stipulation: until Crane had shown that he was in earnest about turning over a new leaf, no one was to know that he was Ella's nearest living relative. And as Crane proceeded to create as bad a reputation in Red

Rock as he had elsewhere—drinking, lying, chasing women
and welching on gambling debts—Mac became ever more
insistent on that point.

This matter of relationship had been given an exag-
gerated importance by Mac, no doubt; yet Brant did not
find it difficult to understand. Not any weakness in Ella,
but the fierce protective tenderness of the husband who
adored her made it seem necessary. Mac had not asked
himself whether or how well she could bear such imagined
"disgrace" as Crane might reflect upon her; rather he had
vowed that she should suffer no slightest annoyance because of his mistake. And it was in his character to shield
her from a vague unpleasantness with the same inflexible
resolution he would have shown in the face of an immi-
nent and deadly peril.

"Last Wednesday night Ralston wanted to talk to me in
private," said Ella. "I met him on the other side of town
near the Johnson house. He claimed to have received word
that he was about to be arrested for forging ten thousand
dollars' worth of checks to pay gambling debts, which was
an item he had never mentioned before. He wanted me to
ask Mac to square things for him again. I refused. I begged
him not to go to Mac. I even cried, I was so upset."

Worth's shaggy eyebrows met. "He was lying, Ella. He
wasn't afraid of being arrested. Rigby was one of his shady
friends and they cooked up that story to get money from
Mac. Reckon Crane was getting sick of Red Rock and
wanted a stake to leave on."

"I suspected something of the kind. . . . The next afternoon Ralston phoned and wanted to talk about it some
more. I arranged to meet him in the watchman's shack at
the mill because Mac wouldn't have liked it if we were seen
together. Ralston was going to Mac himself if I wouldn't
go for him. I tried to stop him—tried to hold him back

by main force—but he went into the mill. There wasn't anything more I could do, so I left him there."

Brant was beginning to see how, from that sly criminal scheme of Crane's, tragedy had developed with deadly speed. Ella would have missed its beginning, having left the mill too soon. . . .

Mac shifted his position in the bed, bracing his wide shoulders more solidly against the pillows.

"Now that we're letting our hair down all the way, you might as well know everything you came to find out, Ed. Andy knows some of it, but not all.

"Crane found me, all right. He came blustering up and said it would be too bad for Ella's reputation in these parts if I didn't get up ten thousand and as much more as was needed to square a cop who was on his way. He was smart in some ways, but he wasn't smart then, because I'd been fed up with him for weeks and was trying to think of a way to get rid of him. I'd already thought of offering him a regular remittance to go to Africa or the South Seas and stay there.

"I didn't give him a chance to finish his piece. I busted him in the face. He was game to fight—I'll give him that much credit—and we traded quite a few punches. Then I slipped or tripped and hit my head on the floor and everything went black.

"The next I knew Andy was shaking me. The chopping machinery had been turned on and Crane's cap and mitt were on the floor and there was blood on the side of the conveyor. It looked as if Crane had gone through."

"How perfectly awful!" Ella exclaimed weakly.

Mac grinned. "It didn't seem awful to me, not the way I felt. I figured we were finished with him for good and I was glad."

Complications had begun to pile up that night when Charlie King, drunk and reckless, came to the office where

Mac was working late, insisting that he had seen Mac shove
Crane into the log conveyor and start the machinery. Mac
was in no frame of mind to pay blackmail to a man who
could not be trusted. He took the revolver from his desk
drawer, intending to frighten King, but King grabbed for
it and the shooting was as Mac had described it to Brant.

"I tried to make it out an accident to keep it from worrying Ella. I don't know who killed King, but it must have
been Crane or Rigby.

"That one, Rigby, came here next day and said he knew
from King all that had happened to Crane. He wanted twenty-
five thousand dollars to keep his mouth shut. I was too sick
to wring his neck, and besides Ella was in the next room, so
I said I'd pay him off as soon as the bank opened Monday.

"But I got madder and madder as I thought it over.
Andy told me he thought Crane was alive and it struck me
that maybe I was being rooked in two ways. That night I
got out of taking my sleeping pills, and as soon as the coast
was clear I got the revolver and started out. I was going to
find Rigby and make him talk. I was going to get the truth
out of him or kill him. Only I wasn't in as good shape as I
thought. I got down the front steps, but I couldn't get any
farther. If Ella hadn't rescued me I'd have passed out in the
snow and that would have been my finish."

There was a minute in which no one spoke. Ella smiled
and said, "You should have told me, Mac. I'd have understood and helped."

He reached out and took her hand. "It's over now."

Again all of them were silent. Then Brant was aware of
Ed Worth speaking.

"If it ain't over," the sheriff was saying, "it's so close to
it there's hardly any difference. Simpleminded as I am, I
can figure this one out.

"Crane and Rigby would have settled for ten thousand
at the start, if you'd fallen for that cheap badge and fake

warrant, Mac. But when you passed out in the mill Crane saw how he could play dead and fix it for Rigby to go after bigger money. He put blood on the conveyor, dropped his cap and mitt, turned on the machinery, swiped Jim Scott's cap and beat it.

"But Charlie King saw Crane leave and was smart enough to know something was wrong. I reckon he caught up with Crane at Maggie's and Crane offered him money if he wouldn't tell. But when King got some of Maggie's white mule in his belly he got a brainstorm of his own and went to see you, and wound up shooting you. Crane must of followed King from Maggie's and choked him to death when he found out what had happened."

"And Rigby killed Crane, eh?" Mac put in.

"Sure," Brant agreed. "You told Rigby you'd pay off and he didn't see why he should split with a man who was supposed to be dead anyway." He hesitated, aware of a vague warning in his brain, as if he was overlooking some small but significant detail that must be fitted into the puzzle before it would be complete. But nothing else came to him, and he finished lamely, "That's how it was."

"We'll get Rigby right away," Worth said.

Ella went to the door with them. She put her hand lightly on Brant's arm, delaying him. "What do you think of Mac now?"

"I wouldn't have believed he could improve so much in one night, or you either."

"That story you and Carol made up has worked wonders. We're going to Palm Beach as soon as he's well enough. I had to get some things at the drug store last night and ran into Carol. It was the first chance I'd had to thank her for playing her part so perfectly. I guess you hadn't told her that I knew it was all a put-up job. She seemed surprised. . . ."

He clung to the edge of the door miserably. "Surprised, eh?" he said. It seemed a totally inadequate word. Now that Carol knew the truth—and not from his own cowardly lips—she must despise him nearly as much as he despised himself.

He would have given anything—everything—to make it different.

19

Ray Saunders was dozing again when Brant and the sheriff arrived at the hotel, and this time there was a witness. Nordquist, the proprietor, leaned against the corner of his desk and grinned.

"Wide-awake bunch of peace officers we got here in town," Nordquist observed inevitably.

Worth did not reply. He strode up to the deputy and cuffed him soundly. The sleeper awoke with a cry, staggered to his feet and raised his fists.

"What the—?" He blinked. "Oh, howdy, Ed. You sure gave me a start. I wasn't looking."

"I'll say you weren't looking. You been asleep ever since Andy and me left here an hour ago. By God, Ray—"

"Now hold on, Ed. I was right here where I should of been. I just sort of nodded this minute." He appealed to Nordquist. "Wasn't I awake all the time up till the last ten seconds?"

"I wouldn't know rightly," said Nordquist, still grinning. "I just come back from church. They was people dropping off there too before Reverend Wirta got finished with his sermon."

"If anything has gone wrong, Ray . . ." Worth left the rest of it hanging in the air and made for the stairway,

with Saunders following sheepishly at his heels and Brant
bringing up the rear.

The sheriff halted in front of the door of Rigby's room,
placed his ear close to the center panel and knocked. He
listened for a quarter of a minute, then knocked more
loudly. Finally he tried the knob and kicked at the bottom
of the door.

"You see, Ray? Just because you couldn't keep awake—"

"Oh, forget it!" Irritation flared in the deputy's tired
voice. "I'll turn in my badge. I'll get a job where they treat
a man like a human being and give him time off to sleep."

"Don't be an idiot. Go downstairs and get a key to this
room from Nordquist. I got a hunch Rigby didn't get very
far."

Brant said, "Saunders heard him snoring an hour or so
ago. Maybe he took something to make him sleep and it
hasn't worn off yet."

"I'd hear him breathing," Worth objected. "Not a sound
behind this door now. If he's inside he must be dead. No
way he could of gone out except through the lobby or
through the window."

"If Rigby is dead, you and I might just as well lie down
and die beside him, Ed. It'll blow our whole cases to pieces."

Again a faint warning pricked Brant's brain. What had
he missed in his mental rehearsal of the known facts re-
lating to the crimes? Was it possible that someone as yet
unsuspected was involved in them, and he had glimpsed
but not quite understood a clue pointing to that person?

He began to pace the corridor nervously. Passing the
door of his own room, he noticed a triangle of white
paper protruding from beneath the door. Saunders' feet
were pounding back up the stairs as he stooped and drew
out an envelope on which his name was written.

"Here's a duplicate key," Saunders panted. An instant
later metal grated in the lock of Rigby's door.

Brant slid his thumbnail under the sealed flap of the envelope. Who would put a note under his door in preference to seeing him personally or telephoning him? In a second he would know—

The sheriff yelled suddenly, "God A'mighty, Andy!" It was the first time Brant had ever heard Worth's tones crack and go shrill as a woman's. Worth was in Rigby's room and Saunders was in the doorway, and the latter kept repeating inanely, "It can't be! It can't be. . . ."

Stuffing the envelope in his coat pocket, Brant reached the others in half a dozen powerful strides. He knew before he entered the room that he was going to look upon murderers' work for the third time in three days, but he was unprepared for the horror that met his eyes.

Peter Rigby had died in the center of his disordered bed with his face buried in the mattress, his arms clasped around his head, his pudgy body twisted half out of loose pajamas that had been a flat blue but now were splotched and spattered with shining crimson. His skull had been smashed as Crane's had been with a hammer or the butt of a revolver, and the pillows and the wall beside them were streaming with the blood that had spurted beneath the many merciless blows.

"It happened just in the last few minutes," said the sheriff, watching a fat drop of gore slide sluggishly down the wall. He touched one of the dead man's wrists. "He's as warm as you or me."

Saunders croaked, "You better take my badge, Ed. I didn't have no idea anything like this could happen, or else I'd of stayed at the top of the stairs and, never shut my eyes once."

"Keep your badge," Worth said gently. "I didn't have any idea either. I could of swore in another deputy to keep watch so you could get some sleep. I didn't have any call to make you stay up all day and all night and all day again, Ray."

Self-reproaches were all very well, Brant thought—heaven knew he had been indulging in them liberally since yesterday—but it was time someone did some investigating. He lifted the pillows gingerly and peered beneath them, then looked in the drawers of the dresser and in Rigby's clothing and suitcase.

"He had a revolver, Ed. It isn't here."

"A revolver? Then that was the weapon—"

"It must have been." Brant pointed to a bloody towel lying in a corner. "When Rigby was dead, the killer wiped the gun and took it with him. Look out for bullets if we corner him."

"There's bullets in my gun," Worth said grimly. "What bothers me is how are we going to corner him? He might be up here in one of the rooms or he might of gone out. Maybe he belongs here in the hotel."

"Eric Nordquist," Brant said softly.

"Huh?"

"He was snooping in Crane's room—the print of his hand proves it. He didn't take that note Rigby wrote to Crane, but he may have read it and guessed there was money to be made. Nordquist always had a liking for money."

"Hell, he wouldn't do a thing like this. What would be his motive and opportunity?"

"We'd have to establish a motive. Maybe he tried to blackmail Rigby. Maybe Rigby tried to blackmail him, or wanted to put him in the middle for some of the dirty work that was going on. Maybe Nordquist was in with Crane in the scheme from the beginning, and when Crane was killed he thought he was being double-crossed. Maybe—but guessing won't put us any farther ahead. Opportunity is another thing. How about that little while when Saunders was nodding? Nordquist said he'd just come in from church and there wasn't anyone to dispute him, but

for all we know he might have come in ten or fifteen minutes earlier than he said."

Worth rubbed his nose meditatively. "I hate to think it,
but we got to start somewhere. Ray, do you mind staying
here with the body for just a few minutes longer? I'll send
you home soon as I can."

"Take your time, Ed." Saunders shuddered. "I couldn't
sleep a wink if I was in a featherbed."

Brant and Worth descended to the lobby, where Nordquist was already relaxing in his favorite chair. He watched
them beneath drowsy eyelids.

"You look like you was all hot and bothered. Wasn't
Rigby to home?"

"He's in," Worth said shortly. "What we're hot and
bothered about is that handprint of yours in Crane's room.
You told us yesterday you hadn't been there."

Nordquist's eyes grew wary. "You want me to tell you
the same thing all over?"

"No, we know you was there. What we want to know
is—why? What did you see there or take from there?"

"Nothing." The old man's hands curled around the
wicker arms of his chair. "Nothing, 'cause I wasn't in the
damn' room."

Worth glanced at Brant. "You tell him, Andy."

"Rigby was murdered within the last half-hour," Brant
said. "The man who killed him knew about a certain deal
between Rigby and Crane. You might as well know that
Crane has been murdered too, the same way Rigby was.
We aren't saying you had knowledge of that deal, but you
can figure out for yourself what the state police will think
when they go over Crane's room and Rigby's for fingerprints and find yours."

Nordquist swallowed painfully. "They won't find mine.
Somebody else put that mark in Crane's room to get me
in bad."

"The police have ways of telling. Even if you've wiped out that handprint they'll find traces of it with chemicals and cameras. You know how they do those things if you read the newspapers."

For a moment longer Nordquist maintained his denial, then he gave in. He whined, "Why do you pick on me when you know I wouldn't ever do nothing wrong? I lived all my life within three miles of this spot and I never yet was in a crooked deal. All I did was take a quick look in Crane's room to find out what Rigby might of been after. I had a right to know what was going on in my own hotel."

"What was he after?"

"I couldn't see nothing valuable. Clothes and some letters was all. I didn't look very hard though, nor very long."

"How about those letters?"

"Do I look like the kind of man who would snoop in other people's mail? I never read a one of them nor even opened an envelope."

"Fingerprints will tell."

"I'm not excited. My fingerprints won't be there."

Worth took over the inquisition. "How long were you upstairs before Andy and me come in? The reason I'm asking, I want to know if you heard noises."

"The only noise I heard was Saunders snoring. I wasn't upstairs all day. I woke up in my room on this floor at nine, had breakfast in the restaurant and went to church. Fifty people seen me there and will tell you so. I just got back when you two come in. I been right here in the lobby ever since."

"Somebody was upstairs. You don't know who could go up and down again?"

"Everybody in town might of while I was away. Since I got back you two and Saunders is all that went up. Oh, yes—Carol Johnson was coming down just as I got back."

"Carol!" Brant echoed.

Nordquist's head bobbed emphatically. "She was coming down the stairs in a hurry. Now I think of it she had a funny look, like she was mad or wanted to cry. I said hello, but she didn't act as if she heard me."

Brant was stunned. He could not conceive of Carol being implicated in the remotest way with what had been done in Rigby's room. He heard Worth ask the hotel proprietor, "Did you see which way she went?"

"She headed straight across the street. I didn't watch to make sure, but it looked as if she might be bound for the newspaper office."

Brant stiffened. "I'll go over and have a look, Ed. Give me a few minutes, will you?"

"Well . . ." Worth was reluctant. "Three or four minutes maybe. We can't be wasting time after what's happened; you know that."

She might have seen or heard the killer of Rigby, he reflected as he plodded across the street. That could account for her preoccupation and her "funny look." And she might have gone to the newspaper office to telephone the sheriff. . . .

But although he was trying to find excuses for her, the fact that she was near the scene of Rigby's death was not the most immediate terror in his mind. More than anything else he was afraid to face her, to look her in the eye, after the way he had deceived her.

He ducked into the snow tunnel he had dug, and as if his mind were shrinking from grimmer subjects it recalled seemingly inconsequential things about those first violent hours of the blizzard. Quarfield had been the first to clear a path here, but the Snogo had buried it again. Quarfield had joked about being spurred to his labor by the need of whiskey. He had put in a strenuous night, carrying Lola

Tucker home on snowshoes and then visiting the saloons
. . . where Rigby, in his thin shoes and city clothes, was
prowling in search of Crane. . . .

Brant found the door of the office unlocked and an
inch or two ajar. He put out his hand toward the knob—
and at that instant, by some subtle shifting of mental im-
ages, a pattern suddenly took shape in his mind and stood
out in fateful clarity. All at once he knew the name of the
murderer he must deal with, and the knowledge had the
shocking effect of a blow between the eyes.

He pushed back the door and stepped quietly into the
deserted front office. The door to the shop was ajar also,
and at its other side someone was speaking:

"Don't you see, you've already destroyed yourself with
the others? Why not put a stop to this insanity right now?"

The voice was clear and steady, and it belonged to Carol.

20

Brant edged cautiously to the inner door and looked into the shop. He saw Carol standing straight and slender in the coat with the white fur collar and a saucy green hat, her face chalky and her blue-gray eyes defiantly intent on someone out of his line of vision. Brant knew who that someone was even before the snarling command came:

"Get over against the wall!"

"No," Carol said. "I'll stay here."

He opened the door. It swung silently almost until the very last, then creaked as its weight bore down on the hinges. Brant was stretching his arm toward a heavy wrench on a table when the man in the shop whirled and pointed a revolver at him.

"Andy!" cried Glenn Quarfield. "For God's sake, why have you got to butt in?"

The menace of the gun made Brant forget about the wrench. He said, "Put it down, Glenn. This is the end of the road. You'll only make it tougher for yourself."

"You think I'll let them lock me up?" Quarfield's gargoyle face was taut with venomous purpose. "I'll be on that twelve-thirty train out of this hole in the woods. Before anyone finds the pair of you I'll be past catching."

"Then there's no point in killing us," Carol argued less confidently. "You can tie us up and leave us."

"You think I'm crazy?" His lips writhed. "Over against the wall, you two. Turn your backs."

"Just a second." Sweat bathed Brant's body, but despair steadied him. "If you're counting on getting out of town, I not only think, I *know,* you're crazy. Worth isn't dumb; he'll be after you."

The revolver—Rigby's' revolver—was aimed at Brant's chest and the range was less than ten feet. Quarfield rasped, "If you don't get over by the wall I'll damn well shoot you where you stand!"

Without looking directly at her, Brant could see Carol inching toward the door. She might get clear if the killer's attention could be distracted. He would settle for her safety and take a chance on his own.

"You'd better call it a day, Glenn. Worth is on his way over here now."

"Then it'll be too bad for him." He broke off as Carol's foot scraped lightly. "So it's tricks, huh? Okay, you asked for it. . . ."

The revolver swerved toward the girl and Quarfield's finger tightened spasmodically on the trigger.

Brant gave one wild shout—*"Look out, Glenn!"*—and leaped for the printer.

The gun jerked and spat a pointed tongue of gray smoke toward Brant. The detonation rang deafeningly in the machinery-crowded room, but Andy Brant felt no slightest pain, no slackening of his rush. He dropped his shoulder a fraction of a second before his body struck Quarfield's, getting under the arm that held the revolver.

The shock of the encounter hurled them both to the concrete floor. Landing beside the other, Brant hammered his right fist against Quarfield's nose. The printer grunted in pain and swung his arm and the barrel of the revolver slashed across Brant's scalp, touching off fireworks in his brain.

Carol was at the door, screaming, "Help! Help, somebody!" Brant's fingers found Glenn's gun wrist and clung to it for dear life. Quarfield's knee jolted into his groin and Quarfield's free hand clawed at his eyes.

A second time the revolver roared, the bullet striking one of the presses and twanging off. Then there were hasty footsteps and the barrel of another revolver flashing down like a club. Quarfield howled, his weapon clattered to the floor and the fight was over.

"Reckon I come about in the nick of time," said Ed Worth. "You look peaked, Andy."

Brant put his hand to his head and brought it away bloody. He looked at Quarfield, who was sitting up, staring at his dangling right wrist.

"You broke it," he said stupidly.

"Be glad I didn't break your neck. I got a mean temper when it comes to handling murderers and sometimes it gets the best of me."

Carol leaned weakly in the doorway. Now that the danger had passed there was no sign of the defiant courage with which she had faced the man who would have killed her. She was trembling and Brant was afraid she was going to cry.

"Did he hurt you, Carol?" he asked anxiously.

She shook her head. "No. Not him."

"How did you happen to be here with him?"

"I was in the hotel and saw Glenn coming down the stairs. He said he wanted to see me about something important. He was coming here and I followed in a minute or so. I didn't have any idea what he had done."

"You were the only one who saw him in the hotel?"

"I suppose so. There was only Ray Saunders in the lobby and he was asleep."

"There you are, Ed," said Brant. "Quarfield slipped upstairs and killed Rigby the minute the coast was clear.

Not a soul knew he'd been in the hotel except Carol. He thought he'd be safe if he could kill her. When I came in he was getting ready to finish her."

"Then Quarfield was in on the blackmail scheme?"

"He invited himself in." Brant got to his feet and rested his weight against a composing stone. "Let me tell you how I see it. We know why Crane sent for Rigby and how their original scheme took on new trimmings when Crane saw a chance to make Mac look like a murderer."

Worth nodded. "That's right. Keep going."

"Well. I suspect that when Quarfield left Lola at her house that night he must have run into Crane on the way back. Having just killed Charlie King, who would have balled up everything, Crane needed an ally. Rigby didn't know about the latest development and it was important that they get together without being seen.

"Crane offered Quarfield a split in the profits and Quarfield brought Crane here, then went out and found Rigby. How about it, Glenn? Is that how you spent the last part of Thursday night at the office?"

"You're doing okay," the printer muttered glumly.

"I can't say how or why you killed Crane the next night," Brant went on. "I'm pretty sure, though, you did. And whether you did or not you're going to get the limit for killing Rigby. So how about enlightening us?"

Quarfield put his left hand inside his coat and produced a sack of tobacco and cigarette papers. "Roll me one, will you, Andy? I can't manage with this busted wrist. I didn't want to kill Crane, believe me. I had to in self-defense."

Brant began to shape a cigarette clumsily. "You mean he tried to kill you?"

"That's it. Lola left word for me at the restaurant Friday night that she was going to a girl friend's and I got suspicious. Crane was at her place and I thought they might be up to monkey business. I sneaked around to Maggie's at about eleven to make sure. Lola wasn't in, but I peeked through a crack in a blind and saw Rigby and Crane and heard what they were saying.

"Rigby had propositioned Mac and was going to collect twenty-five grand on Monday. Crane said they'd scram soon as the money was paid—get a car and head for another part of the country. Crane said he was in a hurry because he'd had to kill Charlie King and didn't want to be nailed for it.

"Crane had been afraid King would double-cross him. He followed King to the mill, heard the shot that got Macfarlane and saw King run out. When Crane found out what had happened he hit King with a hammer and choked him. He didn't know he was leaving the body in the middle of the street where the Snogo would turn it up—he thought it wouldn't be found for a long time."

Quarfield accepted the lumpy cigarette and leaned toward the match the sheriff held. Worth said, "What did that have to do with you?"

"Then I heard Crane say to Rigby. 'Maybe I better kill Quarfield too. I hate to pay him off and he'll squeal his head off if we run out on him.'

"That made me good and sore. I waited till Rigby went away, then tapped on the window and called Crane outside. All I wanted was to have an understanding with him and make sure I didn't get left with the dirty end of the stick, but the first thing he did was try to slug me with a hammer. I took it away from him and slugged him instead. I was so mad I kept hitting him till all at once he was dead. Then I threw the hammer away and shoved him down in the snow."

"That brings us to Rigby," said Worth. "Did I remember to warn you that anything you say can be used against you?"

"It don't matter. I'm up to my ears and I might as well get my hair in it. I knew I'd have to kill Rigby to be safe, but I wanted to wait till he'd got the twenty-five grand, so I could be safe and rich too.

"Yesterday I told Rigby that Crane had decided Maggie's wasn't a good spot any more, and I'd fixed him up in a cabin in the woods. I said we'd arranged for me to take Rigby to the cabin when the money was paid, and Rigby believed me.

"But when you dug up Crane I knew I could kiss that dough good-bye. My only chance was to kill Rigby before you started asking him questions, because he'd put the finger on me sure as shooting. Ever since I left the courthouse I been hanging around the hotel watching Saunders, waiting for a chance to get upstairs.

"When Saunders dropped off to sleep I got the chance. I'd of got out with nobody seeing me, only Carol happened to be going upstairs just when I was coming down. I was about crazy. I decided I'd have to kill her. After two killings another one don't seem so bad. I got her to come here and then Andy showed up—and that's all."

Worth said, "Get up and I'll walk you to the jail to keep Nowka company. You can see Lola there before I turn her loose. It will be your last chance, I reckon." He looked gravely at Brant. "Funny how you were right in the beginning about there being two murderers in Red Rock. I'd get a copy of them Bar Association figures, only there wouldn't be much sense in it now that both the varmints are out of circulation."

Brant could think of only one small item that was still unexplained. What had taken Carol into the Northland Hotel at the precise moment Quarfield had chosen for his escape? He turned to ask her, and was astonished to find that she was no longer in the room.

"She eased out quite some time ago," Worth said. "Reckon our talk was strong stuff for a young gal to be listening to right after she'd come within a whisker of getting killed."

Thrusting his hands into his pockets, Brant frowned. It wasn't like her to leave without saying anything to him, without giving him a chance to say anything to her. Granting that she had cause to hate him, she might at least have acknowledged his service in saving her life.

His fingers touched the envelope he had found under his door. He brought it forth and looked again at the inscription, and realized that it was in Carol's handwriting.

Hastily extracting the folded sheet of paper, he read:

> *Dear Andy,*
> *I'm sorry I was such a fool, but it was partly your fault for not making yourself clearer, so don't laugh at me too much. You can keep up the game by telling Mac I've gone to Detroit to buy my trousseau, and he'll be all healed up before he learns I'm not coming back. With all my heart I wish you happiness and success.*
>
> *Carol*

For a long minute Brant was blind to everything but a vision of her face, now sober and demure, now grinning impishly, now shining. He knew at last that he had mistaken the nostalgic memory of a campus romance for love, and had accepted the counterfeit so long and so unquestionably that when the real thing came he had not recognized it.

Into his chaotic thinking the deep-throated whistle of a train intruded urgently. Then he was running—hatless, with his hair a bloody tangle—leaving Ed Worth and the prisoner to stare after him uncomprehendingly.

He caught the platform of the last car as it slid out of the station. Stumbling through the narrow aisle, pulling himself along by the brass handles of the backs of the red plush seats, he looked for a saucy green hat. There were three passenger coaches, and he found what he was looking for in the last one he entered.

She sat by the window staring at the shabby storm-racked town as it moved past. He said, "Scoop, my darling!" and her eyes came around, muddled with tears. He said, "I'll jump off and risk breaking my neck if you want me to," and she blinked and shook her head.

"Well, then, here we go together." He sat beside her, fumbling for her hand, asking humbly, "Do you think you could put up with me all the way to the end of the line?"

Her voice was little more than an off-key squeak and a sniffle, but there was nothing uncertain about it.

"All the way, Andy," she said.

About the Author

Donald Clough Cameron (1905-1954) skipped college and jumped into the newspaper field at the age of seventeen (as a crime reporter for the *Detroit Free Press*), before becoming a writer in the 1930s. His middle name came down to him from the English poet, Arthur Hugh Clough. He wrote short stories, comic book stories (co-writing the story that introduced Alfred as Bruce Wayne's butler), and six detective novels before he died of cancer. He was survived by his wife, Eva, and a son.

MURDER'S COMING

GRAVE WITHOUT GRASS

BY
DONALD CLOUGH CAMERON

Also Available
Coachwhip Publications
CoachwhipBooks.com

THE CASE OF THE ADVERTISED MURDER

MINNA BARDON

Also Available
Coachwhip Publications
CoachwhipBooks.com

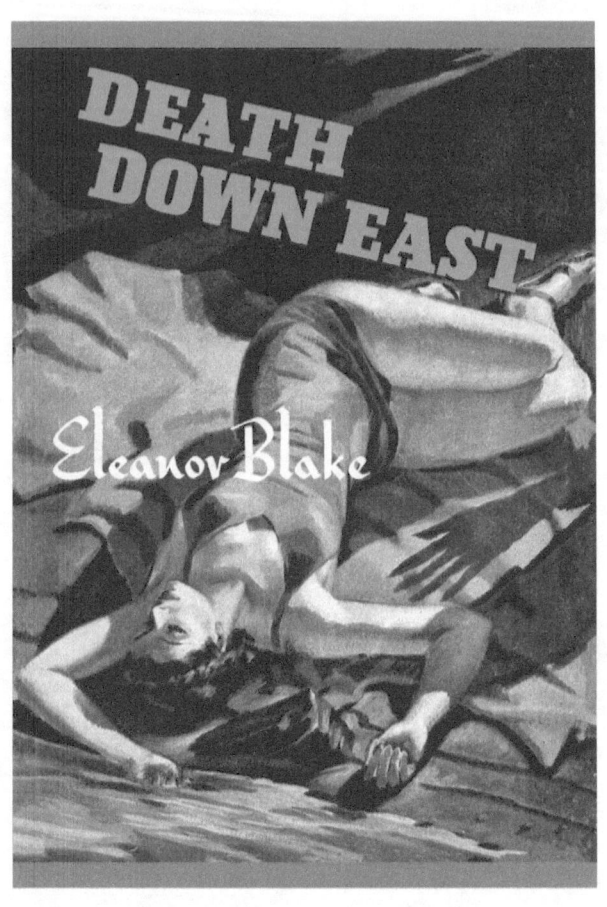

Death Down East

Eleanor Blake

Also Available
Coachwhip Publications
CoachwhipBooks.com

HIDE AND GO SEEK

with, GOING TO ST. IVES

HOTEL

COLVER HARRIS

Also Available
Coachwhip Publications
CoachwhipBooks.com

HELEN BURNHAM

THE MURDER OF
LALLA LEE

THE TELLTALE
TELEGRAM

Also Available
Coachwhip Publications
CoachwhipBooks.com

VIRGINIA RATH

THE ANGER
OF THE BELLS

**Also Available
Coachwhip Publications
CoachwhipBooks.com**

DEAD
WEIGHT
ADDISON
SIMMONS

PATTERN IN BLACK AND RED

FARADAY KEENE

Also Available
Coachwhip Publications
CoachwhipBooks.com